THE FAMILY STORYTELLING HANDBOOK

How to Use Stories, Anecdotes, Rhymes,
Handkerchiefs, Paper, and Other Objects
to Enrich Your Family Traditions

Anne Pellowski

Illustrated by Lynn Sweat

Macmillan Publishing Company
New York

Collier Macmillan Publishers
London

By the same author

The Story Vine: A Source Book of Unusual and Easy-to-Tell Stories
from Around the World

Special thanks to Gay Merrill Gross and Ruth Stotter
for their help in compiling the stories in this book.

Macmillan Publishing Company
866 Third Avenue, New York, NY 10022
Collier Macmillan Canada, Inc.
First Edition
Printed in the United States of America

10 9 8 7 6 5 4 3 2 1

The text of this book is set in 12 point Times Roman.
The illustrations are rendered in pen-and-ink.
Designed by Constance Ftera

Library of Congress Cataloging-in-Publication Data
Pellowski, Anne.
The family storytelling handbook.
Bibliography: p.
Summary: Discusses storytelling as a form of family entertainment,
offers suggestions on how and when to tell stories, and includes
examples of stories for family members to tell.
1. Storytelling. 2. Libraries, Children's— Activity programs.
3. Family recreation. [1. Storytelling. 2. Family recreation]
I. Sweat, Lynn, ill. II. Title.
Z718.3.P44 1987   027.62'51   87-7981
ISBN 0-02-770610-9

To the new arrivals in my extended family:
Matthew, Katie, Rachel, Mia, and Aaron

Contents

Acknowledgments

Selections by Don Davis (pp. 1–2), Norma Livo (p. 15), Kay Stone (p. 16), and James S. Goodman (p. 23), copyright © *The National Storytelling Journal*, Jonesborough, Tennessee; reprinted with their permission and the permission of the respective authors.

Selection on page 36 from *My Father's Daughter* by Mabel Segun, copyright © 1965, African Universities Press (Pilgrim Books), Lagos, Nigeria; reprinted with their permission.

Selection on pages 40–41 from "Nova" transcript of conversation with Richard P. Feynman for the program "The Pleasure of Finding Things Out," No. 1002, copyright © 1982 WGBH, Boston; reprinted with their permission and the permission of Richard P. Feynman.

Selection on page 50 by Frances Clarke Sayers, from the article "From Me to You," copyright © 1956 *Library Journal*, New York; reprinted with their permission.

Selection on pages 25–26 by Patricia Wrightson, from "The Geranium Leaf," copyright © 1986 *The Horn Book Magazine*, Boston; reprinted with their permission.

Selection on page 5 by B. F. Skinner and M. E. Vaughn, from *Enjoy Old Age: A Program of Self-Management*, copyright © 1983, W. W. Norton, New York; reprinted with their permission.

Selection on pages 48–49 by Jane Yolen from *Touch Magic*, copyright © 1981 Philomel (Putnam), New York; reprinted with their permission.

Story on pages 29–30 by Jasper and Pippin Hitchcock, reprinted with their permission and the permission of Kim Lew Kee.

My deepest gratitude to Cecile Beijk van Daal, M. van Zahdvek, Joke Thiel-Schoonebeek, their families, and numerous other persons in the Netherlands who shared their memories of handkerchief stories.

Thanks also to Dr. Margaret Mary Kimmel, Naomi Siegel, and Bonnie Frederick of Pittsburgh, for permission to recount personal anecdotes; to George Shannon of Alaska and Wisconsin, for background information on storyknifing; and to Dr. Glending Olson of Cleveland for permission to paraphrase some paragraphs from his book *Literature as Recreation in the Late Middle Ages*, copyright © 1982, Cornell University Press.

THE
FAMILY STORYTELLING
HANDBOOK

PART ONE

Why Tell Stories

Telling stories is among the least costly and yet the most effective means of entertainment available to any family. The satisfaction level that storytelling provides for teller and listeners alike can be enormously high, for many reasons:

1. Storytelling creates an intimate, from-me-to-you feeling that is hard to match in any other form of entertainment.
2. Family stories can be personal, immediate, and unique, helping to build the special identity every person needs.
3. For centuries and centuries, stories have been the best means of explaining and passing on the moral values a family or people wishes to retain.
4. Stories can show that there are others in the world who have different values, and that toleration of these does not have to diminish one's own sense of right and wrong.
5. Storytelling can be healthy and therapeutic.
6. Telling stories is fun!

In the past, many families shared stories as a matter of course. Don Davis, a minister and storyteller from North Carolina, describes the natural way in which he heard stories:

As a child I spent a lot of time in the home of my Grandfather and Grandmother Walker back on Fines Creek in Haywood County. In my earliest memory, they lived in their "old house," a hewn two-story log house (still standing) with a wonderful, cold spring just outside the back door. There were giant rocks above the house (which backed against the mountain), and a view out the front, across the arrowhead field to the ridge on the other side of Rush Fork Gap.

. . . Sometimes in the late afternoon, Grandmother would take me and my Aunt Bonnie (my mother's youngest sister) and sometimes my cousins Andy and Kay, and head up the mountain. We would carry along a black frying pan and some of Grandmother's sausage and eggs.

We'd walk way up in the steep pasture and pick out a good, big boulder of a rock. Then whatever kids were there would hunt all around for firewood while Grandmother or Bonnie took what we found and built a little fire in a hollow of the rock. After it was going, we would break the eggs into the pan in which the sausage had been already cooked and broken up, and scramble the eggs and sausage all up together and have a one-dish supper.

Gradually it would get dark, and we would walk home in the dark and go to bed in Grandmother's big, deep featherbeds.

On days like this, storytelling was going on, but we didn't know it. There was no formal time set aside as "story time" or any real separation of story from the total fabric of conversation. Story was the language of normal communication and the natural result of talking, as much as going somewhere is the result of walking instead of standing still.

. . . I never said "tell me a story" for I never regarded these events as "stories" but as simply hearing about real things that had happened. Instead I would say, "tell me about old Whitebear (my favorite)," or "tell me about the time Jack climbed that tree and met that talking wolf." It is hard for me to give names to stories, for they were not known by name, but rather as "the time when. . . ."

That kind of life is past, you might be thinking. True, the rural life with its emphasis on extended families and with its different pace is experienced now by only a small percentage of our population.

Yet achieving these qualities of shared intimacy is possible among modern urban families as well. "Story time" might be available only for a few minutes each day, and confined to the smaller, nuclear family, but the family that is willing to try storytelling may find that those minutes become priceless.

Many older persons can remember tales told by a grandparent, uncle, aunt, or other family member. Younger persons are more likely to recall stories told by a teacher or librarian, because family storytelling suffered a decline in this century, especially after the arrival of television. However, there are many signs that telling stories in a home or family setting is once again on the rise, in many parts of the world.

Even with all their access to modern, sophisticated entertainment, the children and young people of today still like to hear stories told to them directly by a live person. The many storytellers like myself, who tell professionally in schools, libraries, museums, theaters, or other places, have graphic proof of this hundreds of times a year.

In my own family, I spent countless hours telling stories to my seventeen nieces and nephews as they were growing up. Now that they are parents themselves, they beg me to tell the same stories again, for their own enjoyment and for sharing with their children.

Veteran storytellers Ellin Greene and Laura Simms conducted an extensive project teaching storytelling among a group of mostly urban children. When the young people were asked "What would happen if there were no stories in the world?" they gave some surprisingly perceptive answers, as recorded in the *Chicago Journal*, May 26, 1982:

Said one child: "People would die of seriousness."
Another replied: "When you went to bed at night it would be boring, because your head would be blank."
Still another answered: "There wouldn't be a world, because stories made the world."

Another reason for telling stories is that the process of telling them or listening to them keeps us healthy! Many psychologists have pointed out the benefits of storytelling. The mutual buildup of trust and intimacy that occurs between teller and listener can last far beyond the confines of the actual place and time of telling.

The most dramatic example I have ever encountered was a case I heard about from Dr. Margaret Kimmel, professor of children's literature and library science at the University of Pittsburgh. Ever since her years as a children's librarian with the Enoch Pratt Free Library in Baltimore, Maggie Kimmel has been a storyteller, and although she is now a professor, she still frequently does storytelling with large and small groups of children.

She always opens her story sessions with a very effective device that she learned from her first storytelling teacher, Sally Fenwick of the University of Chicago. To describe in mere words the way in which Maggie uses the device simply cannot convey the effect it has on most audiences. Suffice to say that it involves an imaginary magic circle, into which the listeners are first drawn and out of which they are later released.

Dr. Kimmel described to me one occasion when she told the story "Sody Sallyratus," from Richard Chase's *Grandfather Tales,* to second-graders in an inner-city school on the East Coast. As usual, she opened and closed with the magic circle device. A few days later, one of the children who had been at the story session was involved in a traumatic and tragic event. When found, the child was murmuring the refrain from the story "Sody Sallyratus" and spoke about being in the "magic circle."

The school psychologist called Dr. Kimmel, and after they had discussed the case, they agreed it would be best if the child, by being reminded how Dr. Kimmel had done it, could be helped to release himself from the "magic circle." This he did successfully, and, as far as is known, he did not resort to this magical escapist device again. But it did seem to serve him well at the moment he most needed it, when the real world overwhelmed him, through no fault of his own.

The behavioral psychologist B. F. Skinner believes that storytelling can give dignity and respect to those entering old age. His book *Enjoy Old Age: A Program of Self-Management*, which he co-authored with M. E. Vaughan, contains much excellent advice on all aspects of old age. This is how storytelling is recommended:

4

A small repertoire of string figures, paper foldings, and magic tricks, carefully husbanded, will confer status. Jokes, verses, and conundrums will spice a youthful conversation. . . . Good stories are never told enough for the very young.

But above all, these two authors conclude, conserve your energy and your stock of tales. If children are enjoying themselves, leave them alone.

The conviction that stories are hygienic (good for one's health) and therapeutic (healing) does not date from modern times only. There are a number of references in ancient texts that indicate such concepts of storytelling were quite the accepted thing. In the early Greek play *Heracles*, Euripides has the character Amphitryon say to his daughter-in-law Megara, who is awaiting the return of her husband:

Be calm;
dry the living springs of tears that fill
your children's eyes. Console them with stories,
those sweet thieves of wretched make-believe.
    —Lines 97–103, translated by Gilbert Murray

In the late Middle Ages, when stories were beginning to be read as well as listened to, there were several commentaries about the power storytelling can exert on the development of the healthy person. Glending Olson, a professor of English literature at Cleveland State University, has translated a number of documents from this period that show that storytelling was recommended as part of the upbringing of children. In his book *Literature as Recreation in the Later Middle Ages*, Professor Olson cites, among many others, a Latin manuscript titled *Tacuinum Sanitatis* (Tables of Health), a translation of a thirteenth-century Arabic manuscript by Ibn Buttan.

This manuscript recommended that all families should have access to a "confabulator," or storyteller, who would have "good discernment in knowing the kinds of fictions in which the soul takes delight." Furthermore, it was recommended that the "confabulator" be a person who knew not only true "histories of great princes" but also "delightful stories that provoke laughter." Presumably, to be healthy one needed a good mix of stories that showed actions or morals one was supposed to imitate and stories that were meant to be pure fun.

I personally tell stories for all of the reasons I have mentioned, but the chief one is that I enjoy doing it. To hear waves of laughter and gasps of surprise from the audience, to sense the deep involvement (sometimes noisy, sometimes completely quiet) as people share the story I am telling and live through it with me, is to experience something so satisfying that I am willing to risk much time and effort to be able to do it again and again.

PART TWO

When to Tell Stories

Bedtime

Night or evening has been a traditional time for the telling of stories for thousands, perhaps tens of thousands of years. Storytelling is a major form of entertainment before retiring for adults and children alike.

The Latin poet Horace, in his *Satires*, gives a good description of what went on during an evening get-together of friends in ancient Roman times:

> O evenings, and suppers fit for the gods! with which I and my friends regale ourselves in the presence of my household gods. . . . Then conversation arises, not concerning other people's villas and houses, nor whether Lepos dances well or not, but we debate on what is more to our purpose, and what it is pernicious not to know. . . . Meanwhile, my neighbor Cervius prates away old stories relative to the subject.
>
> —Book Two, Part 6, translated by Christopher Smart

One of the stories Cervius "prates away" is the tale of "The Country Mouse and the City Mouse."

In many societies, large, extended families or whole groups of families would set aside a time just before retiring during which stories were told, songs sung, riddles exchanged, or life simply commented upon by the more verbally gifted participants. When the group was lucky, it had among its members one or more persons especially gifted in storytelling.

Anna Spurgarth, who lived in a West Prussian village at the turn of the century, has described how her father entertained the whole village almost every night for eight straight winters (from 1900 to 1908). The stories he told, his daughter relates, were mostly folk and fairy tales, but he also told tales of things that had happened to him. Whoever fell asleep *during* the storytelling had to put a fifty-penny piece in a saucer on the table!

In some wealthy European or Asian families of the eighteenth and nineteenth centuries, there was a special servant or family member whose designated job was to tell stories at night, before the household went to sleep. If the head of household (or someone else of authority in the house) had insomnia, the teller was expected to get up and begin telling soothing, sleep-inducing tales.

In my family, it was my oldest sister, Angie, who told me and my sisters bedtime stories. In my autobiographical novel, *Stairstep Farm*, I have written a number of episodes remembered vividly from childhood. I am "Anna Rose" in this scene; the others are my sisters:

Tonight, Angie told how Pal rescued a girl named Anna. She had fainted on the railroad tracks, just before a train was supposed to come along. Angie's voice went lower and slower as she told the story: "In the distance, the train whistled. Anna did not hear it. She had fainted dead away, with her head across one of the rails. In the yard, Pal looked around. He did not see Anna. He heard the train whistle. Like a shot, he took off down the road that led to the railroad crossing. He came to a high gate. It was closed. Pal had never jumped over such a high gate. Only a horse could do it. The train was coming closer, closer, closer. Pal ran and leaped forward. The gate was too high. He could not even get near the top. Again and again Pal tried, each time jumping a little higher. Clo--ser, clo--ser, clo--ser came the train."

Angie's voice was now a soft, long-drawn-out whisper. Quietly, slowly, she put her hands in her mouth. Suddenly, she let out a piercing whistle: "Wheeeeeee!"

Mary Elizabeth jumped and grabbed onto Angie. Janie pulled the sheet over her head. Anna Rose leaped out of bed.

"What happened?" she cried.

"When Pal heard that whistle so close," Angie continued, "he took one mighty leap, cleared the gate, ran to the tracks, caught hold of Anna by her dress and pulled her off the tracks—just as the train whizzed by. But he couldn't get his tail out of the way in time, so the tip was cut off by the train. And that's why Pal's tail has no tip."

Anna Rose breathed a sigh of relief. She knew it was a made-up story. Pal would never be able to do something like that. But Angie made it seem so real that while she was telling it, Anna Rose was sure it could happen.

My sister Angie does not recall these bedtime story sessions, and they may well have been few in number. Yet they assumed such an importance in my imaginative life that my recollection is of storytelling almost every night.

Parents who wish to begin a regular routine of bedtime storytelling often start with a read-aloud story, followed by short rhymes, verses, or songs. Experts such as Jim Trelease, author of *The Read-Aloud Handbook*, and Margaret Kimmel and Elizabeth Segal, in their book *For Reading Out Loud*, point out that this should begin when the child is an infant, six to nine months old.

For infants, it is a good idea to begin with bedtime stories, songs, and rhymes that are soothing, repetitive, and not too full of dramatic action. The rhyme "Sing a Song of Sixpence," for example, is more suited at first to daytime telling, especially if it is accompanied by tweaking the nose of the child in imitation of the blackbird who snaps off the nose of the maid. On the other hand, rhymes such as the following are ideal for a bedtime session:

These fingers are so sleepy,	*Point to child's hand.*
It's time they went to bed.	
First you, Little Finger,	
Tuck in your little head.	*Bend little finger down.*
Ring Man, now it's your turn;	*Bend ring finger down.*
Then comes Tall One great.	*Bend middle finger down.*
Pointer Finger, hurry,	*Bend index finger down.*
Because it's getting late.	
Let's see if they're all tucked in.	
No, there still is one to come.	
Move over, Pointer Finger;	
Make room for Mrs. Thumb.	*Bend down thumb.*

It is not necessary to use these exact words. Simple phrases and a quiet, pleasing voice are what's essential. After doing a five-finger rhyme, try one on the ten fingers or the ten toes, such as this one. Point to all ten fingers or toes, then wiggle one toe or finger when naming each animal. When completing the final line, put a blanket over the child or turn out the light, to signal it is time to sleep.

Down on the farm at the end of each day,
All of the animals politely say:
"Thank you for treating us so well today."
The cow says: "Moo."
The pigeon says: "Coo."
The sheep says: "Baa."
The lamb says: "Maa."
The hen says: "Cluck."
"Quack," says the duck.
The dog says: "Bow-wow."
The cat says: "Meow."
"Neigh," says the horse.
The pig grunts, of course.
Then the barn is locked up tight.
And the farmer says: "Good-night!"

Later, when such rhymes have been used frequently, and the child has shown that they are recognized and appreciated, rhymes with more dramatic action can be added to the bedtime story session. However, it is always a good idea to close with those that suggest it is time to wind down and go to sleep.

For those adults who can't remember the rhymes, and don't feel particularly inventive in making up new ones, an extensive collection can be found in the paperback book *Ring A Ring O' Roses*, available from the Flint Public Library, 1026 East Kearsley, Flint, Michigan 48502. Send a stamped, self-addressed envelope and ask for price and other order information for the current edition.

At bedtime, any of the well-known repetitive stories, such as "The Three Bears" or "The Three Little Pigs," are enjoyed by children from the time they are quite young; I have told them to children as young as fourteen months. But in most cases the children had heard at least six months of recitations of the simpler Mother Goose rhymes, and had been read aloud to from numerous very simple picture books, such as the flap books of H.A. Rey and the books about Spot by Eric Hill.

There is nothing wrong with reading stories aloud, instead of telling them. Indeed, research now shows that reading aloud on a regular basis to children between the ages of two and seven is probably the most significant factor in preparing them to be good readers. However, I believe it is also important to do some purely oral storytelling. Only in this way do children see the verbal playfulness and imaginative responses that can be called forth from within each person as well as from without, by using books, recordings, films, and other media.

A regular bedtime routine can consist of five or ten minutes of quality time, just before the child is put to sleep for the night. This should be sufficient to begin with. The time can gradually be increased to fifteen minutes, and then go on up to a half hour. As the child matures and becomes more adept at using words, the bedtime story session can also include a story told by the child to the parent. Starting at age three or four (or even earlier, if the child is especially verbal), the parent might begin the bedtime story session, and then ask: "Would you like to tell me a story about something that you heard about or that happened to you today?" Later, this can be shortened to: "Would you like to tell me a story?"

Beginning at approximately three or four years, most children are ready for simple folk tales, either told or read aloud. At age five or six, the bedtime story hour can include a fairy tale or two, and perhaps a read-aloud chapter from a longer book, to be continued each night. Again, the child might be invited to contribute a tale.

But the bedtime session should always be brought to a close by a story or song or something related by the parent. Sometimes it can be effective and appealing to select a short rhyme to say as a closing, indicating the light will be turned out and it will be time to sleep. Here is one example:

> Snip, snap, snout!
> The story is out!
> And so is the light.
> Good-night!

Around the Campfire

The campfire seems to bring out the storyteller or the story listener in many of us. Perhaps it is some elemental response, inherited from our prehistoric ancestors, that demands sharing a story when we are seated together in a circle in the dark, with the flickering glow of a fire alternately illuminating the faces of those around us or casting them in shadows that suggest they are full of mysterious possibilities. The effect of the stories told during such sessions is generally one of shivery, even horrifying delight. That is, we can be truly frightened, so that all the physical signs of fright show up, yet at the same time so reassured by the presence of the fire and familiar people that the overall feeling is one of tremendous relief: We have faced the fear or horror and conquered it rather than let it conquer us.

The person who tells stories at such nighttime sessions must be very sure of the audience. If the story is truly scary, the listeners must be given some sign that they can trust the teller to lead them out of the terrors of the tale to a satisfying ending. Should the story end on a note of fearful ambiguity, the teller must be certain that the audience is mature and experienced enough to handle an open-ended conclusion.

For most modern-day children, such storytelling experiences are encountered in scouting groups, while away at summer camp, during slumber parties, or while staying overnight at a friend's house. The campfire is sometimes symbolic—a flashlight under the covers, for instance, or hands held in a circle in the dark. Fortunately, much of the telling in such cases is by one's own friends and peers, or by those only a few years older.

Once, when lecturing in Australia, I was invited by members of a storytelling group in Canberra to join them and their families on a picnic barbecue. After we had eaten and played a round of cricket, we went to a very large national park nearby. It was getting late in the day, and suddenly we noticed that a group of the children had somehow or other gotten separated from the rest of us. They were not small children, but ranged in age from eight to twelve.

Since the park was surrounded by a fence, we were not too concerned at first; however, it began to get very dark, because a storm cloud was approaching. The parents then had a very anxious hour before they could organize teams of searchers and locate the children, who were indeed lost in the vastness of the park. But once they realized they were lost, the children had had the sense to stay put. When found, it was obvious they were all scared, but not abnormally so. We asked them how they had spent the long hour waiting for the searchers to get to them, and the oldest girl answered: "Telling stories."

I happened to be in the car with that girl on the way home, so while sitting next to her in the backseat, I asked her about some of the stories she knew and liked. She proceeded to tell some of the most horrifying, spooky, and supernatural tales I have heard, relating them as if they were stories of actual events that had happened to actual people she knew.

Her mother was aghast. She asked if these were the stories the children had been telling each other during their ordeal of waiting and wondering (She must have had visions of the nightmares they would have for weeks). But the daughter said, in a very matter-of-fact tone: "Oh, Mother, of course we only told funny stories or things that would make us laugh."

Yet for the rest of the ride home, the girl continued to relate the most bizarre and terrifying tales. It was as though during the fearful waiting period she had kept up the spirits of the younger children so they would not panic, but now, going home in the safety of the family car, she needed to exorcise all thoughts of the dreadful possibilities of what could have happened. And she did this best by naming or identifying them in stories.

While Traveling

Who has not seen children get bored, restless, and cranky during the tedium of a long trip? It never ceases to amaze me how few adults have discovered the method that makes the time pass most swiftly for young and old—namely, storytelling or reading aloud from an engrossing book.

I like to tell stories illustrated with tricks performed with string or a handkerchief or some other object, so I am almost never without such a collection of items in my pocket or purse. Many a transatlantic flight has seen me put them to good use. One flight, to London from New York, I remember particularly well. I had been seated next to a woman and her four-year-old daughter, who was upset about having to leave her daddy behind. She decided to show this by throwing a tantrum. I simply took out my nesting doll set and launched into a story.

A few dozen stories later, the child finally fell asleep. At the end of the flight, the mother thanked me profusely. But a businessman and his wife, seated in the row behind me, invited me out for a night of theater and dinner in London, in gratitude for the peace and quiet they had had on the flight. I accepted on condition they would each promise to learn a story to tell the next time they faced such a situation.

Many of the stories I use in such circumstances can be found in my book *The Story Vine*. I also use some of the stories in Part Five of this book, because they are equally well suited to the task of keeping children occupied while in a confined space.

Norma Livo, a Denver storyteller and teacher, has had many similar experiences, especially when traveling with her own family. She writes:

On a recent camping trip with my daughter, Lauren, and her two children, Todd and Jody, and my own son, Kim, there were many chances for quality story sharing.

During one meal when there were no clean spoons, five-year-old Jody was given a grapefruit spoon with a wooden handle and serrated edge. Of course, she fussed and fumed, saying the spoon was ugly and that she would not eat with it. Then Uncle Kim told her a sad story about a beautiful princess who ate off a golden plate, with a golden knife, fork and spoon: *One day while the royal family was out gathering huckleberries in the woods, the princess got lost from the rest of the family. After wandering for a day in the woods, her dress was tattered, her dainty slippers were torn, and she was hungry. That night, she came upon the campfire of an humble traveler who was heating some stew over a fire. Seeing her plight and not knowing she was a princess, he offered her some hot stew in a tin bowl with a tin spoon. The haughty princess stomped her foot and declared that she would not eat with such a spoon. She demanded a golden spoon. The traveler shrugged his shoulders and said, "Well, suit yourself." The princess starved to death.*

When Uncle Kim asked Jody, "What is the moral of the story?" Jody grinned slyly, knowing what Uncle Kim expected to hear, and said, "The moral of the story is to always carry your golden spoon with you."

Everyone laughed and Jody was teased considerably the rest of the trip. When we got home, I bought a small golden spoon and had Grandpa George drill a hole in the handle. We attached it to a golden chain and gave it to Jody. She now has a golden spoon ready for all future outings.

Some persons use their travels as the basis of stories, then tell the tales once they are home. Sometimes these can stretch into very tall tales, as Kay Stone, a Winnipeg teacher and storyteller, can attest:

My awareness of the powers of the spoken word grew from my early childhood as I listened to my father's voice spinning out tales from books, from his own father, and—most wonderful of all—from his imagination. His life was not any more unusual than other fathers' but he had the ability to weave marvelous stories from everyday events. His most enticing tales were inspired by a year-long job delivering gasoline to remote stations in the Florida Everglades in the late 1940's. During his lonely hours of driving, he told himself stories, then retold them to my sisters and me when he returned home. I can still picture the incredible animals he "met" decades ago—the snakes that stretched from one side of the Tamiami Trail to the other, the alligators as huge as his Texaco gasoline tanker, the two giant owls who tried to carry off that tanker and the Everglades mosquito who intervened. Ah, history. Lies they may be, but they brought to life an otherwise unreachable part of my own history and prepared me for the exploits of Greek heroes and other adventurers.

Ruth Stotter is a professional storyteller who travels a great deal, both for her work and for personal enrichment, and to accompany her husband on his business travels. She wanted to find a simple story that could work in virtually every culture, and that would be easy to learn in a few basic phrases, in almost any language. Her choice of favorite traveling story is given on page 102.

My recommendation to any person who does a great deal of traveling is to learn a few short, surprise-ending stories, especially those that use some illustrative device, and to tell them at least five or six times. They will then be fixed in memory, ready to be called up when needed. The string, handkerchiefs, origami paper squares, small dolls, or other objects that one might wish to use can be kept in a corner of a briefcase or purse. The bit of space they take up is more than compensated for when one discovers how much of a relaxation response they can call forth. In addition, illustrated stories allow a perfect stranger to enter into meaningful communication with others without knowing much of their language. The moment you bring out such stories and share them, you are sure to get a number of other stories in return.

Family Reunions, Picnics, or Gatherings

Many families organize reunions on a regular basis; others do it only every five or ten years, or sporadically. Advance planning allows far-flung members to participate in this bonding experience. It can also allow for some wonderful family story sharing.

A few years ago, some six hundred descendants of my paternal great-grandparents gathered at a location near the Wisconsin farm where the original homestead, dating back to the 1860s, is located. I cast the family history in story form, which my brother and I narrated while others panto-mimed the action as a kind of pageant. This was one of the highlights of our reunion weekend.

Just this summer, our family had another reunion, but much smaller this time; it was planned by the seventeen grandchildren of my parents. Many of them are now married and the parents of young children. Each of the seventeen was given a questionnaire to fill out, asking for suggestions of activities to include at the reunion. I was delighted to see that my nephew Rob put this suggestion on his return: "Have Aunt Anne tell the story 'Cheese, Peas, and Chocolate Pudding' and follow this with a cheese, peas, and chocolate pudding lunch!" He had loved this story as a three-year-old, and, of course, he loved it when his mother went along with the nonsense and made such a lunch. Now that his son was the same age, he wanted to renew his acquaintance with the tale and have that experience again.

I am the storyteller at most family functions, but whenever we have a large family picnic, my sister Mary takes over. Many years ago, when her boys were Cub Scouts, she had learned to tell the story "Going on a Lion Hunt." She told it at a family picnic, and it was such a success that she was asked to retell it whenever we had such summer gatherings of the extended family. Then her children and their cousins grew up. Now she is sometimes asked to repeat the tale, with its audience participation, for the next generation of children.

Wakes for the dead have often been an occasion for storytelling in some cultures. This gives the survivors a chance to tell or listen to tales about the person they have lost; it is a very healthy part of the mourning process. When children have to face the death of a relative or classmate or some other person close to them, one of the aids one can use in this adjustment period is the telling of stories.

Animals who die are often deeply mourned by children, and it can be therapeutic to tell stories about some of the things the child remembers that the pet did. Humorous or dramatic events are often the easiest to describe. Some children like telling or writing their own stories about pets who have died.

Marriages and anniversaries can also call forth stories. How refreshing and entertaining it is to hear, at the time of the toasts to the bride and groom, a short, well-told story followed by an appropriate toast. Family members who find it difficult to express their emotions of love and affection on such occasions can do so through the medium of storytelling.

The twenty-fifth wedding anniversary of my oldest sister and her husband took place while I was doing some storytelling research on the tall tale. Thus, at the party, it seemed only natural that I retell the story of their meeting, courtship, marriage, and family in this style, exaggerating all the details I could remember. Their ten children got into the act and suggested further things to add. It was one of our most hilarious family parties, still remembered by all who were there.

There will usually be much informal, light storytelling and joke exchanging going on as a matter of course on such occasions as family reunions or gatherings. However, don't forget to include some serious stories of family history when they are called for. A fine example of such storytelling can be seen in the film *Yonder Come Day*. In it, Bessie Jones of St. Simon's Island, off the coast of Georgia, teaches her grandchildren and great-grandchildren the games and songs and stories that her ancestors invented to help ease the burden of being slaves.

She also tells the tale of some ancestors who simply could not continue to bear a life of slavery, and who leaped to their death by drowning. Mrs. Jones actually takes the children to the site when they are of an age to understand the story (they appear to be in their early teens) and there tells the story in a simple, understated way; she does not add a message or moral. The effect is memorable and immensely moving. These young-sters will surely come to appreciate both the joys and sorrows of their ancestral past.

Holidays

Some families have elaborate rituals associated with certain holidays. These rituals have often developed over more than one generation and are passed on as a kind of sacred trust. Such families would no more think of changing their ways of celebrating the holidays than they would of chang-ing their name. At most, they will modify the rules a bit.

Other families operate at the other extreme: They have almost no tradi-tions associated with specific holidays. Such days are spent in activities no different from any other day that is free from work and school.

For a large number of families, holidays are filled with tension or with a vague uneasiness that the family should be doing more to mark the day in special ways. These families are often involved in special activities that have been selected by parents or other power figures, or activities that have been chosen arbitrarily, because everyone else in the neighborhood is doing them or because they have been touted as fashionable things to do. Children may or may not go along with the activities, creating further strain.

There is nothing intrinsically right or wrong about celebrating holidays in the same way or in a different way each year. What parents and grand-parents should have fairly clear in their own minds is the meaning that the holiday has for them. Only then can they attempt to pass on the values they associate with the holiday.

One of the best ways to do this is through stories about the persons and/or events associated with the holiday, these stories should be introduced long before the children enter school. Reading aloud from books or docu-ments can add to the celebration, but the basic story and meaning of the holiday should be told in the parents' or grandparents' own words, beginning in simple terms when the child is very young, and getting a bit more complex each year.

Here is an example of how it might be done.

On the morning of the Fourth of July, Abby, who is thirteen months old, is seated at the breakfast table with her parents. Her father or mother says something like this:

> It's the Fourth of July today, Abby (*point to calendar*). It's Independence Day. This is the day our country got its independence a long time ago. We like living in a free country. We're going to celebrate. We'll go to the parade. We'll wave our flags. Then we'll go on our picnic. And tonight we'll celebrate by watching the fireworks.

Abby might well not understand a word of this. The next year, when Abby is twenty-five months old and able to speak quite clearly, one of her parents repeats essentially the same story as above, possibly stopping to ask Abby if she can count to four, and repeating the names Fourth of July and Independence Day. Her mother might add this:

> A long, long time ago your great-great-great-grandparents used to live in Poland. They decided they wanted to come to this country so they could have more freedom. They liked to celebrate the Fourth of July, too. They had parades and picnics, just like we do.

When Abby is a little more than three, she has a new baby sister, Rachel. The same story is repeated, with a few more details added. Rachel listens in and gets what she can out of the telling. After Abby's fourth birthday, the story can be expanded again. However, the first parts should be kept simple and direct, for Rachel. Mostly for Abby, the following might be added:

> When our country became a new country, they decided they had to have a president. The first president was George Washington, and the second one was John Adams. President John Adams had a wife and her name was—Abigail! And that's who you are named for, Abby. For Abigail Adams, the wife of President Adams. She was there when they had the very first celebration on the Fourth of July.

In this way, the story can grow bit by bit, with the parent going on as long as the child seems interested. The repetition each year reinforces not only the information, but the genuine interest on the part of the parent and the patriotic or other feelings that are invoked on such a holiday.

Of course, there will be some parents who, for one reason or another, don't feel particularly patriotic on such holidays. In such cases, it is better to hide the negative feelings until the children are older and better able to deal with the darker side of our political history.

If you live in an area where other national, ethnic, or religious groups celebrate their own traditional holidays, those are perfect times to introduce your child to tolerance of customs and beliefs that are different from those accepted in your family. At the table, or after seeing a news account on TV covering such a holiday, tell something positive that you know about the group or people whose holiday it is. It should not be preachy or told in such a way that the child gets the message "you'd better like them, or else!" Make it a short story about a person you admire who is from that group, or an interesting tale you have heard.

For older children, try to recall some revealing story about yourself that tells why you feel the way you do about a holiday, and why you want them to celebrate it with you. In the end, such stories will be far more effective than any nagging or coaxing to join in the celebration just because it's always been done that way in your family.

Religious Ceremonies or Celebrations

Because so much of religious ritual is complex, it has been written down on scrolls, cloths, or manuscripts, then printed in books. This makes us associate formal religious life with reading. But there is much oral tradition in religion as well. Only recently has there been extensive, serious study of the role of storytelling in passing on religious beliefs and rituals.

One has only to think of the power of the parable to realize that stories can make a lasting impression on moral development. For some people morals are tied in with religious belief, and they look for every opportunity to use parables with children and young people, in the hope that this will teach them to live by the values of their professed faith.

Once, on a plane returning to the United States from India, I sat next to an Indian man, who asked me what my profession was. When he found out that I told stories to children for a living, he began to describe to me the stories that he had been told as a child, by an elderly relative.

He expressed the conviction that these stories were what taught him how to live his Hindu faith, and lamented the fact that urban Indian parents no longer told these stories to their children. "And they are not written down," he insisted. "Those stories were so unusual, I have never seen them in a book."

I questioned him further, asking him to recall as many of the plots and motifs as he could, and he complied. In fact, he spent the better part of the flight telling tales. I did not tell him so, but I recognized virtually every one of the motifs and plots he used; they were all familiar to me from my years of studying worldwide collections of stories. And yet, he was telling the truth when he said he'd never seen them in a book, because the *way* in which he'd heard them told—the conviction of the teller in getting the message across—cannot be found in the bare bones of those stories as they are printed.

That is how stories should be used in a religious context—not just rote readings from a prescribed text, but tales told in such a way that the listeners recognize the teller truly believes what he or she is saying.

For Christian families, the obvious times for telling stories are at Christmas, Easter, and the periods of Advent and Lent leading up to those two feasts. Less obvious are the feast days of saints; yet there are many stories associated with them. I will never forget one of the legends associated with St. Nicholas, because of the circumstances under which I heard it.

I was a Fulbright exchange student in Germany some thirty years ago. On the second Sunday of Advent, which that year was St. Nicholas Day, I went to visit a friend who rented part of an apartment belonging to a widow and her two children. I inadvertently went in the wrong door and walked in on the family, seated around a table on which two candles of the Advent wreath had been lit. The mother was telling (and the children were raptly listening to) the legend of St. Nicholas and the boys he saved from being boiled to death. She did not allow my entrance to interrupt the story, but continued on to the end. The dim, eerie light; the simple yet dramatic manner in which she told the tale; and the gruesome motifs—everything combined made the story seem not preposterous but plausible.

Jewish families also have numerous holiday traditions that are complemented by storytelling. In the introduction to his lovely book of Hanukkah stories, *The Power of Light*, Isaac Bashevis Singer describes how his father, a strict rabbi, always preached to his children and rarely allowed them to play games. But on Hanukkah they could play with the *dreidel*, and he would tell them stories.

In another book, *Naftali the Storyteller and His Horse, Sus*, he mentions how he loved to listen to his Aunt Yentl tell stories on the Sabbath, after the main meal. His aunt was such a good storyteller that even Dvosha, the cat, liked to cock her ears and listen!

In a recent "Souvenirs" column in *The National Storytelling Journal*, James S. Goodman reminisced about the way in which he came to associate the Sabbath with storytelling, because of the tales of his grandfather:

> [He] told me about the great adventures of the Jewish heroes and martyrs, stories from the Bible, and tales about his own youth when he traveled the country as a vaudevillian, with a trumpet strapped to his back. He told of mystery and magicians and great teachers who traveled modestly from town to town, to places where my Grandpa had never been.

Moslem families, particularly those from Sufi tradition, have wonderful stories as well. There is usually a tale to fit almost any specific situation. Many of these are permeated with a delicious sense of humor.

Moslems, Buddhists, Hindus, Confucianists, and believers in other Asian religions have specific times to tell both religious and ancestral myths and stories. Most children who grow up in such families are aware of oral traditions from very early on. Families who follow Baha'i, Unitarian, or Ethical Culture Society teachings generally want to introduce the stories from all the world's religions, since they believe one can learn to become a moral human being by following virtuous examples found in all of them.

There are many good collections of stories to use on holidays, both secular and religious. Luckily, both adults and children can hear such tales brought to life by professionals in libraries, museums, theaters, and other places, because many storytellers are invited to perform specially for the holidays.

However, for home storytelling, the personal experience story that matches religious holidays is probably the best and most meaningful, for both the teller and the listeners: one more step forward in our attempts to live our lives by the values we say we profess.

Other Special Times

Children's birthdays often call for parties, and some parents prepare lavish food, gifts, and entertainment. Others prefer more modest celebrations. In either case, few people think of telling stories at such parties, as a break in the boisterous schedule of games, favors, and fooling around.

You might try to settle down a group of youngsters by placing them in comfortable chairs in a semicircle, then telling them a story or two. Depending on the age of the children and their interests, the stories could be spooky, humorous, dramatic, or a combination of all three.

If you feel at ease telling stories to your own child or children, but don't feel you can cope with a group of their peers, consider hiring a professional storyteller for the party. Most cities now have such persons, who perform for a fee. They can be located by consulting the *National Directory of Storytelling* or the folders on child entertainment that can often be found in your local public library.

Other parties—for both adults and children—can sometimes be enlivened by an infusion of storytelling. Baby and wedding showers, going-away or retirement parties, graduation days—I have told or heard stories (usually hilarious ones) on all such occasions.

Spontaneously

Adults should not feel they must wait for a special day or occasion to tell stories to children. There are moments on many ordinary days that call for storytelling, if only one learns to recognize them. This is especially true when one is around very young children, who are insatiably curious and still rather egocentric. They may already like stories and rhymes read to them from books, but they have yet to experience that first flash of recognition that occurs when you see yourself in a story.

Patricia Wrightson, an Australian writer for children, has captured such a moment very well, and the reasons why one should tell a story at precisely that moment:

> Maybe you've been lucky enough to listen while a mother tells her toddler its first story. The toddler would have to be quite tiny, and the story is probably about something that has just really happened: "Once there was a little girl called Jane, and she had a puppy. It was a greedy puppy. Jane put her cookie on the chair, and the puppy came and ate it up." Jane whimpers, and her mother quickly makes the ending come out right. "So Jane's mother gave her another cookie, and she ate it all up, and the greedy puppy didn't have any." Jane may sit quietly for a while in an inward-looking trance or she may bounce up and down demanding more or she may launch into a chanting, incomprehensible story of her own. What she never does is look bored or confused or dissatisfied by this wholly new sort of experience.
>
> Jane knows story on sight. It's an instant extension of self—an immediate part of her world. . . .
>
> Jane's story will never be the subject of serious critical study, but it

has given her a sudden, rich gift. It has taken an experience of hers, something she had only felt, and given it shape and definition; now Jane can see what happened as well as feel it. She can see, reassuringly, that the outcome was all right and the experience fitted into life. As she sits in her inward-looking trance, seeing the cookie and the puppy again in her mind, Jane is inheriting man's second world—the one in the mind. She is seeing with clarity what isn't there, even in a picture—a truth, an actuality, that now exists only in the mind. And even more than that: the stinging injustice of being robbed by her own puppy didn't happen to Jane in isolation; someone else was there and saw and understood. She wasn't alone.—*The Horn Book*, March/April 1986, p.179

That's all well and good, you may be saying, but *my* children are already beyond that stage; most of them are in school. How do I get started with stories with *them*? They lead such busy lives, one has to schedule an appointment to get any private time with them.

This is all the more reason for trying some spontaneous storytelling in periods when you are together: in a car on the way to do shopping, waiting in a doctor's or dentist's office, at mealtimes, or when a child is recuperating from an illness. There are quite a number of opportunities, if you really look for them. Once you get into the habit of using time for a short story, you will find yourself resorting to storytelling again and again, even to the extent of giving factual information you want to convey by putting it in story form.

On the spur of the moment, encourage your older children to tell you stories, either ones they have heard, or made up, or read in books. Open by saying something like: "I saw you reading a book the other day, with an interesting cover. What was it about?" Or, for a still older child: "I noticed you were reading——(here you can name almost any classic or well-known contemporary book). I read that so many years ago, I've forgotten the story. Remind me what it's all about."

Above all, never let a storytelling opportunity pass by. If you are one who regrets not having had the experience of hearing your own parents and elders tell stories, then make a conscious effort to rectify that with the next generation. Tell them stories now!

PART THREE

What Kinds of Stories to Tell

Stories Based on Family Events

The most important stories to tell in family circles are those that only the family can know and pass on. These include birth and death stories, high or low points in the family history, humorous (even vulgar) things that have happened to one or more members of the family, and stories that explain why a family does things in a certain way, lives in a certain place, and the like.

What is the most important story for each child?

I am convinced that the single most important story that each child hears is his or her birth story. The sense of being wanted or unwanted, of being an individual with interesting characteristics or just another statistic with no personality, of knowing who one is and one's place in the world or of feeling lost—all of this is conveyed most deeply in the way in which parents tell a child he or she arrived in the world (or the way in which they avoid the subject altogether).

Many current child-rearing manuals explain to parents how they can tell their small children about the facts of birth. Some of them give very explicit directions as to how to answer the child who questions "How was I born?" However, very few of them mention the fact that, although the child is curious about the physical explanation, he or she also probably wants to know about the emotional aura surrounding the event. Children want to be reassured that their parents were excited, hopeful, and, finally, happy that they arrived.

What are some examples of birth stories?

One of the most beautiful examples of parents telling a child his birth story occurs in the film *Blonde Venus*, starring Marlene Dietrich and Herbert Marshall. The next time this is shown in your area, or on late-night television, watch at least the first part. Observe the manner in which the two parents describe to their son the loving and fairy-tale-like world into which he arrived, and the joy and specialness he brought into their lives. Of course, the story is told by two consummate actors assuming roles, but it is done in such a convincing way that for those few minutes, one is sure this is a real situation, and that the family with such a store of love and intimacy will live "happily ever after." We suspend disbelief even though we are already aware of the fact that all is not well in the parents' relationship. This child, we are sure, will grow up knowing who he is and how deeply he was wanted; it will sustain him all his life.

A birth story does not have to be as fanciful as that to be successful. It can be a simple recounting of such facts as the time of day the birth occurred, what the parents were doing, some silly or serious or surprising thing that happened just before or after the birth, the manner in which a name was chosen, the reactions of siblings or other family members, or any number of similar details. For an adopted child, of course, the story is concerned with the day of arrival into the adoptive family and all the events leading up to it, as well as things that happened afterward. Mrs. Mobi Ho is a mother who beautifully describes the importance of these seemingly ordinary facts:

> Not long ago, at my five-year-old daughter's request, we went through photographs of her since birth and arranged them in an album to "tell her story." Several times since she has asked me to "read" the album to her. I point to her at two weeks, still a tinge of pumpkin after a struggle with jaundice. We talk about the silky skin of newborns and a fragrance which reminds our midwife of turnips. We laugh together at a photo of her at 10 months, swaggering around with a sock in her mouth.

Each time we look at these photos, I realize how deeply my daughter trusts me to be a reservoir of memory for her, to recall the things too shadowy for her to recall and to interpret the cycles of her young life.

At the Hillcrest School in Toronto, I met Jasper Hitchcock, who is half Chinese-Canadian and half British-Canadian. He told me an intriguing story he and his twin brother, Pippin, had evolved, regarding their Chinese family name.

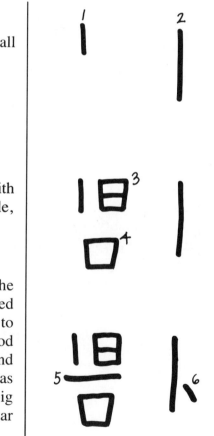

Once, long ago, there was a small river[1] and a big river.[2]

Nearby there was a small village[3] with a road running through the middle, and next to it, a big village[4].

One day an evil dragon made the small river overflow, which flooded the small village. The people ran to the big village. They asked their God to build a dam to stop the water. And so the God did.[5] The evil dragon was furious and into the air he tossed a big piece of the dam, which landed near the big river.[6]

Water started to gush through the hole in the dam, just missing the big village.[7] The dragon attacked the God, who took out his sword and defeated the dragon, sending him away except for his tail, which the God buried in a corner of the small village[8], as a reminder to others.

The God then built three more dams on the small river[9] and three more dams on the big river[10]. He looked back at his work and saw the name "Bik Yook." And from that time on the land was called "Bik Yook."

小
碧

碧 玉

There have been other instances when children have volunteered to tell me the story of their names. But all too many times, I will comment on the beauty or originality of a child's name, and ask how he or she came to have it, and the child does not know. We should all possess at least a short story about our names: why we have them, and what they mean.

Should you wish to introduce long-ago periods of family history to little children, who have almost no concept of the length of years or decades or centuries, try experimenting with the device of the nesting doll. These are wooden dolls from Russia, Poland, or other parts of central Europe that fit inside each other. If you have such a set of dolls, you might use them in this manner.

(Show biggest doll): This is your great-great-great-grandmother. Her name was Louisa. She didn't call herself "Louisa." She was born in Poland, and in Polish her name was Leocadia. She came

across the ocean to America, in a big ship. Then she came by train from New York to Wisconsin. That was a long, long time ago.

(Show next size of doll): This is your great-great-grandmother. Her name was Marianna. She was born in a little sod house in Wisconsin. She could walk right on top of the roof of her house, because it was built against a hill. There were trains near her farm but she never went on one.

(Show next size): This is your great-grandmother. Her name was Anna. When she was a little girl, she went everywhere in a horse and buggy, because there were no cars then. She didn't get to ride the train, either.

(Show next size): This is your grandma. Grandma's name is Angeline. All her life your grandma has lived on a farm. She still lives on a farm, doesn't she? And she likes to drive the tractor. But she has never been on a train.

(Show next size): This is your mommy. Do you know her name? Yes, her name is Kathy. She likes to take you for rides in the car, or on the train.

(Show smallest size): And this is—who? Yes, Kyla, that's who. And soon Mommy will take Kyla on the train to visit Grandma, and she can tell you more about Great-Grandmother, Great-Great-Grandmother, and Great-Great-Great-Grandmother *(Put dolls back inside each other as you do this).*

If you prefer, you can tell about family members in one generation, rather than several. On page 107 there is another kind of story to tell with nesting dolls, based on a folk tale rather than family history.

If you feel you do not know enough about your family's history, try to locate an elderly relative or two who might help you recover some of the stories before they are lost. Even though this might be a relative you have never been particularly close to, you will generally find that most people like being asked to "pass on their wisdom and lore." There are now handbooks that explain how to do this so that the results are satisfying to the person being interviewed and the one doing the interviewing.

Or, consider taking a short course in genealogy or oral history, to help you learn the skills of tracking down your past. Whether you delve into only the more recent past, or get hooked on genealogy as a hobby and try to go back several centuries, you are sure to find some intriguing and entertaining family stories.

Traditional Folk and Fairy Tales, Myths, Legends

In the twentieth century, fairy tales (and their close relatives, folk tales and myths) have had their ups and downs. There have been decades in which they were championed and other decades in which they were downgraded, or even vilified. This usually happened because of the changing attitudes of educators and parents. Some believed fairy tales were of little value to children, or even harmful. Others were convinced that the strong response that fairy tales brought out in most children was an indication that they had key importance in child development, yet they weren't sure exactly why.

What does psychology have to say about the fairy tale?

Psychologists have, for the most part, recognized that fairy tales can be powerful forces in the development of the personality. Freud himself did not write much about fairy tales, but a number of psychologists who follow his general principles of analysis have explored at length the meaning of fairy tales. Bruno Bettelheim is the best-known of these, and his book *The Uses of Enchantment* is perhaps the most extensive examination of the symbolism inherent in fairy tales when looked at from a Freudian viewpoint. Bettelheim advocates using fairy tales with children because "more can be learned from them about the inner problems of human beings, and of right solutions to their predicaments in any society, than from any other type of story within a child's comprehension."

Jung, in contrast to Freud, wrote a great deal about the themes, characters, and actions found in fairy tales and myths, all around the world. He believed many of them were expressions of the "collective unconscious," his term for memories, thoughts, and feelings shared by all of humankind. Many of Jung's followers place great stress on the importance of keeping these myths and fairy tales alive through use, not only with children but with adults as well. It is one of the ways, they believe, that humans can liberate their emotions.

Behavioral psychologists have been generally more skeptical about the positive power of the fairy tale. Some of them believed that children were encouraged to withdraw too much from the real world by reading or listening to fairy tales. They also speculated that some childhood fears were enhanced or exaggerated by fairy tales, instead of being relieved by them. Still others believed that children who were suggestible might imitate the violence and questionable ethics in some of the fairy tales.

What do educators of today say about the fairy tale?

There is still much disagreement, but there seem to be more teachers in favor of the fairy tale than in previous decades. More and more research has shown that, just after they begin to sense that there *is* cruelty, deception, and instability in the world, children need a chance to withdraw safely from the realities and regain their equilibrium. They search for the order and authority of their early years, when their parents (or other authority figures) appeared to know everything and could always make things come out right. Often, they find this in the fairy tale.

Also, the language of fairy tales is full of simple beauty and homey, yet poetic, imagery. The experience of listening to the flow of such words and phrases is pleasing, quite apart from the meaning and action they convey.

Adults escape from reality by reading romances, or watching soap operas or other fictions on television. Most of them have no difficulty, once the book is closed or the TV set turned off, in coming back to the real world. In the same way, children need opportunities for daydreaming and withdrawal from the pressures of daily life.

When do children like fairy tales?

Generally, the years from five through eight or nine are the times when most children want and need fairy tales, or escapist literature of that type. Some children begin to like them later; a few not at all. The fairy-tale phase generally lasts no more than two or three years, but there are some children who continue to like them until they are ready for the reading of modern fantasy or science fiction, of the type adults like.

Often, if parents have told and read aloud many kinds of stories to their children from the age of a year or so, they will recognize quite easily the moment when children are ready to move from stories like "The Three Bears" or "Henny Penny" to such stories as "Little Red Riding Hood" or "Jack and the Beanstalk," and thence on to even more complex stories, such as "Cinderella," "Puss in Boots," "The Twelve Months," or "The Wild Swans."

How does a parent select fairy tales to tell or read?

For those parents who heard such tales told to them as children, there is little difficulty in selecting and passing on stories to the next generation. Most often the stories are remembered with such pleasure that the parent can't wait to try them out. Some parents will go out of their way to search for precisely the versions they heard when young, because they are convinced those are the best.

Other parents have a harder time finding just the right fairy tales to tell at the different stages of a child's life. In such cases it often helps to consult a children's librarian or a teacher, especially one who has extensive experience in reading aloud or telling such tales to a wide variety of children. Each child is unique in his or her response to fairy tales, but there are some general patterns that can be noticed. If you can describe your child's likes and dislikes, chances are that a qualified, experienced children's librarian will be able to select some appropriate fairy tales for you to read and tell.

What if my child is frightened by fairy tales?

If you have chosen well, even those stories that have some violent or dreadful event in them will not be frightening, except for passing moments. In most cases, children need and want a certain amount of scariness, in the years from about six and up. They want to show that they have learned to conquer their fears, or they want to identify with some hero or heroine who has done so. If you leave out all the terrible things from fairy tales, then you must also leave out the great good things that can conquer this terror: courage and resourcefuless in the face of evil, sacrifice that can bring well-being and happiness, faithfulness to a belief or a person, and many more. And it is just these qualities that all of us most need to see in our heroes and heroines.

Above all, use common sense. If a story frightens and disturbs you a great deal, making you worry about your child's reaction, do not use that story. You are almost certain to pass on the fear. It is not a good idea simply to change the story, or to take out the elements you do not like. Your child may come upon the story someplace else, and may then wonder all the more about the parts you left out. It is better to select another story. There are hundreds of fairy tales, and you are sure to find a few that satisfy you and your child.

If your child seems pathologically frightened by tales, it is wisest to consult a psychologist. Chances are the child is trying to show that he or she has some deep-seated fear that needs to be overcome, a fear not caused by the tales, but simply brought to the fore by hearing them.

Stories about the Environment

From an examination of the myths and legends of peoples from all over the world, we can speculate that one of the major purposes of storytelling was to explain or make sense of the environment. The telling of stories probably gave a feeling of control over the environment, as well as expressing a healthy respect for it. Since it was necessary (in terms of absolute survival) to be a keen observer of the subtle ways in which one's surroundings were changed by humans or animals or weather or the like, it was important to train children and young people to recognize these things. This was done by direct, action-oriented training, such as teaching how to recognize the footprints or spoor of humans or animals; by demonstrating the changes in behavior caused by the imminent approach of a storm; or by many similar skills that are still taught today in some traditional societies.

Observation skills were also taught by the use of story. But, equally important, real and allegorical meanings behind observed signs were also taught.

One of the most beautiful and impressive examples of such a use of story can be found among the Ibo people of West Africa. The poet Mabel Segun gives a short version of the tale in her autobiographical novel *My Father's Daughter*.

> We were in our own little world and nobody could interfere with us. We sat there idly watching the clouds flitting by. They looked like cotton wool. I said to Okhen [the girl watching her], "I wish the sky were nearer, I'd like to touch those cotton wool things."
>
> To my surprise Okhen said, "There was a time when the sky was so close you could reach up and touch it with your hand."
>
> "Why is it far away now?" I asked, interested. And then Okhen told me this story.
>
> "Once the sky was very close to the Earth. It was filled with food. Nobody worked in those days. You just had to stretch your hands any time you were hungry and break off a piece of the sky."
>
> "How did it taste?" I asked Okhen.
>
> "Delicious," she said, "because it came from Heaven." She continued the story.
>
> "There was one rule, however, and that was, you should only take whatever you needed for one meal, no more. You were not allowed to store it. Everybody obeyed this rule except for one greedy man who, because he did not work for it, broke off a very large piece. As he was unable to finish this piece he had to store it. But the food became rotten and had to be thrown away. The sky was so angry about this waste that it shot right up, far, far away where no one could reach it. Since then people have had to work in order to get food.

There are many versions of this tale, which I have come across in printed as well as in oral forms. After a discussion with Ms. Segun in which I asked what she remembered as the core truth or meaning of the story, I realized that it represented her people's belief that it was necessary to practice the most stringent control over wastefulness of the bounty of the environment. There might be years when plentiful rains from the sky produced fruits enough to satisfy everyone's hunger. But then there might come a lean time, when the sky yielded almost no rain (when it had moved to its furthest-away point, in allegorical language), and no matter what their efforts, humans would have a hard time finding enough to eat.

Not all of the stories tied to the environment (or even a tiny piece of it) have such broad philosophical implications. Some are merely poetic or dramatic attempts to make us notice the beauty or strangeness or uniqueness of a particular place or thing.

I grew up on a farm in Wisconsin, but it was near the town of Winona, Minnesota, which is situated on a bend of the Mississippi, next to a long, shallow lake that lies in the shadow of a rocky bluff called Sugar Loaf. From infancy I had been taken on periodic trips to Winona, mostly to visit relatives. Such a trip always conjured up excitement, because it meant "going to town." But the real romance of going to Winona did not begin for me until a cousin happened to tell me the tragic tale of the Indian princess We-no-nah, who fell in love with a brave not of her people, but of another tribe. When her father was about to force her to marry someone she did not love, We-no-nah leaped from Sugar Loaf into the shallow waters of the lake below.

I subsequently learned that this legend has been used to call attention to similar rocks or cliffs above lakes in a number of North American places. Yet somehow, after hearing that legend, "going to Winona" has meant much more to me, and still does to this day: It means going to a place where the romantic, however tragic, is possible; it means being willing to take a metaphorical leap over cliffs, past the safety of family and the society one is familiar with, into the unknown.

I was saddened, then, when on a visit to a school in Winona, none of the children in a particular group could retell the legend, or associated it with the name of their town. Was it perhaps that the curriculum called for it at a later grade, and therefore it was not to be programmed into their lives until the system decreed it?

It seems to me far better if we first acquire this poetic and dramatic knowledge about the shapes and spaces of our environment in a family setting. Parents, grandparents, uncles, aunts, cousins, siblings, or family friends can combine to fill in the gaps we have in our perception of what is around us, and most of all, to show us that even though we think we perceive something in its entirety, there always seems to remain something hidden, something elusive.

The distinctive characteristics of flowers, trees, plants, and animals are often celebrated in stories that are very old. Even a generation ago, the number of persons knowing these stories, or at least their bare-bones outlines, was considerably larger than it is today. Who, today, can relate "Why the pansy has a face," or "Why the aspen trembles," or "Why the bear is stumpy-tailed"? Why should we know these stories, you might ask? The environmentalist might answer that we should know these stories if for no other reason than to alert us to notice the diversity and complexity of life on planet Earth. It is very hard to explain the importance of maintaining as much of this diversity as possible if the average person cannot tell the difference between an oak tree and an elm.

Recently, on a trip to Poland we drove through areas of grassy or grain-rich fields sprinkled with poppies. I immediately thought of this legend, first encountered in a German children's book:

> There was once a wealthy merchant who had a son and a daughter. The merchant sent his son off into the world to seek new goods to sell and trade. After a time, word came back that the son was being kept a prisoner by an evil king. "If you wish to get your son back, you must pay a high ransom for him," said the king's messenger. "And, you must send your daughter to be the king's slave." The merchant was so saddened by this news, he fell ill and died.

> "I shall go and free my brother," said the girl. She gathered up all the wealth left by her father and set off. She had to wander many years before she came to the far-off kingdom where her brother was in chains. She did not wish to use the money set aside for his ransom, so she often went hungry. Her clothes were in tatters, and her shoes had long worn out, so she went barefoot. When she arrived at the evil king's stronghold, her feet were bloody and she could hardly speak from weakness. She handed the ransom to the king, and then expired.

The brother was set free, but he wondered how he would find his way back home, for the evil king had taken him by night to a faraway land where he knew no landmarks. He went out of the castle walls, and there he saw a path of bright red flowers, wandering across the fields. He followed it, and it took him in the direction of his home-land, for soon he began to recognize familiar places. He realized then that it was the footsteps of his sister that he was following. Wherever she had stepped and left a drop of blood from her feet, a flower had sprung up, to honor the memory of the selfless girl who had thought only of saving her brother. We call these flowers poppies; they still spring up each year and remind us of love and sacrifice.

The two examples cited thus far might lead one to suspect that all stories explaining natural phenomena are as unrelenting as Nature. There are many stories with sunnier themes drawn from ancestors' musings about flowers, fruits, trees, and such things.

When walking through an orchard filled with ripe, rosy apples, for instance, one might tell a short version of the Roman myth of Pomona and Vertumnis:

Pomona was the only nymph who did not like the wild woods; she preferred her fruit orchard. There she would prune and graft and practice the art of gardening. She kept her orchard closed, and let no men come to woo her. She wished to be alone with her beloved trees.

A young man, Vertumnis, saw her and fell in love with her. But he could make no headway. He would put on disguises so as to get into her orchard: Once he passed himself as a reaper, and another time as a vine-pruner. He could at least have the joy of looking at her.

At last, he made a plan. He came to her disguised as a very old woman, offering to help her pick the fruit. At first, it did not seem strange to Pomona that the old woman should say things like: "You are more beautiful than any of these fruits." But when the old woman kissed her, in a way no old woman would have done, Pomona was startled. Then she listened as Vertumnis spoke to her softly: "Do you see that elm tree over there, with the grape vine twined around it? See how different they are? And yet they support each other well. Are you not like that vine? You would like to stand alone, but you could be so much more if you did not turn away from those who desire you. You are willing to listen to an old woman, yet not to young men. But there is one who loves you more than the rest—Vertumnis. You are his first love, and his last. He too cares for your gardens and orchards. He would work by your side."

Vertumnis went on, telling Pomona about other lovers, and what happened to them when they were unfeeling or careless. At last, he dropped his disguise and stepped forth as a radiant youth. Pomona blushed, so impressed was she by his eloquence and beauty; she yielded to his pleas. And from that day, her orchards had two gardeners. To this very day, many orchard fruits are called pomes, after the beautiful Pomona.

As with all stories, do not expect immediate and positive response to stories about the environment from every child. Be prepared to accept the fact that children's tastes and interests differ; some will like very detailed stories of the environment, and will become keener observers by honing their skills while listening and looking; others will prefer more prosaic tales; still others will prefer mostly traditional fairy tales, with their own make-believe environment, and a logic that is strict, but that does not match that of the scientific world.

In an interview he did some years ago for the television program "Nova," the scientist Richard P. Feynman pointed out how he discovered a wide difference in taste in his own two children:

I got a kick, when I was a boy, of my father telling me things. So I tried to tell my son things that were interesting about the world. When he was very small, we used to rock him to bed, you know, and tell him stories. I'd make up a story about little people that were about so high would walk along and they would go on picnics and so on; and they lived in the ventilator. And they'd go through these woods which had great big long tall blue things like trees, but without leaves and only one stalk. And the . . . had to walk between them and so on. And he'd gradually catch on that this was the rug, the nap of the blue rug, and he loved this game because I would describe all these things from an odd point of view.

And he liked to hear the stories and we got all kinds of wonderful things. He even went into a moist cave where the wind kept going in and out; it was coming in cool and went out warm and so on. It was inside the dog's nose that they went. And then, of course, I could tell him all about physiology by this way and so on. He loved that and so I told him lots of stuff. And I enjoyed it because I was telling him stuff that I liked. And we had fun when he would guess what it was and so on. And then I have a daughter and I tried the same thing. Well, my daughter's personality was different. She didn't want to hear this story. She wanted the story that was in the book repeated again and re-read to her. She wanted me to read to her, not to make up stories, and it's a different personality. And so if I were to say a very good method for teaching children about science is to make up these stories of the little people, it doesn't work at all on my daughter. It happened to work on my son. Okay? —Transcript of a conversation from the program "The Pleasure of Finding Things Out," "Nova"

When introducing the environment to children through stories, be guided by your own feelings of fun or delight or wonder, by the questions you like to ask and the questions children like to ask you, and by their responses to the stories you do choose to tell.

Purely Entertaining Stories

There are a number of story types that have no message or moral at all, nor are they particularly noted for subtlety of language or uniqueness of character and plot. Nonsense stories, some tall tales, and many of the "trick" stories fall into this category. They are most often used to pass the time, or as "fillers" to provide relief between the telling of tales that are much more meaningful. Also, like so much that is genuine humor, they can give a sense of lightheadedness or euphoria that is infectious.

More than thirty years ago, psychologist Martha Wolfenstein pointed out the value humor has for the young child. In her study *Children's Humor*, she gave numerous examples of funny stories, riddles, and jokes children tell among themselves or to others, and analyzed the role this oral material plays in developing self-confidence. Nevertheless, one can still find many parents and educators who see no purpose to what they call "foolishness."

However, with new research that is testing the therapeutic uses of laughter in helping to cure disease, perhaps the value of these stories will increase: those told by children themselves and those told by adults to children or adults. We should all have a few of them at hand, ready to call on at a moment's notice, if only to save a situation from complete boredom, or to attract the attention of restless young minds.

The British call some of these silly folk tales "drolls," and one of these that I have told for thirty years is "Master of All Masters," from the Joseph Jacobs collection *English Folk and Fairy Tales*. By stretching it a bit, one could say that there is a moral to the story, which can best be paraphrased by the title of a Carl Sandburg poem: "Watch out how you use proud words." However I tell it for the sheer fun of it.

Another type of nonsense story found worldwide is one in which a wife or husband asks a spouse or child to do something quite reasonable, but the person being asked does something perfectly ridiculous instead. The sensible character then gets incensed by the stupid actions of the foolish one, and goes off saying, "I will not return until I find three persons sillier than you."

Recently, in a storytelling class in Pittsburgh, I showed a video of a storyteller narrating one such tale, called "The Three Sillies." We all enjoyed the nonsense of it, especially the part where the wife meets a man who knows only one way to get his trousers on: He hangs them up in a tree and then tries to jump into them.

The very next day, one of my students, Naomi Siegel, was dressing and her husband happened to ask her why she put her skirt on over her head.

She confessed to him that she really didn't know why she put her skirt on by slipping it over her head, instead of stepping into it. She laughingly asked him why he put his pants on the way he did, and then she told him the story of "The Three Sillies." They had a good laugh about it, and her husband was still chuckling about it when he left for work. Naomi left for class. Later in the day, he called to ask her to repeat what the other two sillies did, because he couldn't remember, and wanted to tell the story to a friend!

Another student, Bonnie Frederick, recalled a silly bit of nonsense she and her children have enjoyed ever since they were little; they act it out whenever they think someone is getting a bit too melodramatic. It requires a small bow as a prop:

(*Put bow under nose*)	"You must pay the rent!"
(*Put bow in hair*)	"I can't pay the rent!"
(*Put bow under nose*)	"You must pay the rent!"
(*Put bow in hair*)	"I can't pay the rent!"
(*Put bow as tie*)	"I'll pay the rent!"
(*Put bow in hair*)	"My hero!"
(*Put bow under nose*)	"Curses! Foiled again!"

One of the saddest things I ever heard was from a stern headmistress in a school I once visited, in a country where the culture was rich in oral myth and folklore. But little use was made of this oral material in the national curriculum, and when I asked for stories, especially funny ones, I was told, "Madam, we have no humor in our culture." This proved to be not at all true, but with such heavy stress in the educational system on the use of didactic material, it is likely that much spontaneous humor will die out.

I see so many children whose lives are tragic or depressed, for one reason or another, and one of the small ways I can respond to their needs is by telling them funny or diverting stories. I do so whenever I can.

Stories in Which the Listeners
Appear as Characters

As was shown previously, many parents have discovered how much children like being put into stories as characters. These can be stories based on real happenings, or made-up stories that ask children to use their imaginations and see themselves in new roles.

For such storytelling, one needs a generous amount of imagination and a fairly broad knowledge of folk and fairy tales. The more one has read of this kind of story (or listened to it), the easier it will be to borrow motifs and action, and even language, to use in a reworking of the tale. Sometimes it is possible to take these traditional motifs and put them in modern stories. In any case, the chief characters are given the names of listeners in the audience, and sometimes of the teller as well.

This kind of story seems to appeal most to those tellers and listeners who like wild exaggeration or very dramatic action. Its appeal for me is the chance it gives me to "balance" some of the frequently occurring themes in folk and fairy tales. For example, so many stories focus on the oldest or youngest child in a family. Since I was a middle child myself, I made sure, when telling stories to my nieces and nephews, that I concocted some tales in which it was the middle son, or the second or third daughter, not the youngest, who triumphed over difficult odds.

One factor I have always kept constant is the positive, upbeat ending. Stories can be one way for children and young people to learn that all lives have their disappointments, big and little, but a story pieced together on the spur of the moment, in which the child is a named character, is not the place to attempt subtle messages. Rather, the effect one is aiming for is a triumphant "you did it!"

Stories Inspired by Objects

I frequently ask my audiences to imagine themselves back in very early times. Then I ask: "What do you think early humans used first to tell their stories? Did they draw pictures on the walls of the caves where they lived? Did they sing chants and dance out stories, pantomiming what had happened? Or did they try to tell each other with their voices, and thus developed common words that most of the members of the group then understood? Which came first, in your opinion?"

It is interesting to note that the answers are usually divided fairly evenly among the three choices. Occasionally, one group is so convinced of the correctness of their viewpoint, they will argue vociferously and come up with intriguing suggestions as "proof."

This exercise helps many persons get over the mistaken notion that early storytelling was purely oral, and that it relied entirely on the memory of individual persons who passed it on by reciting or telling. That was the case in many instances, but there are equally well-documented examples of the use of many devices to help storytellers remember complex myths, religious epics, or family or tribal histories.

Pictures drawn on leaves or stone, or in sand, snow, or mud; string knotted or twisted in unusual patterns; bits of bones or shells strung on vines; mnemonic scripts on boards that appeared to be individual languages—all these and more were used by storytellers who felt they needed memory aids.

Recently, a fascinating exhibit at the Brooklyn Historical Society explored the period just after the arrival of the Dutch in the New World. The exhibit was based on the newly translated journals of Jasper Danckaerts, a Dutchman who lived in Brooklyn in the seventeenth century.

Native American groups were still in control of most of the area, and the Dutch had to deal with them. Danckaerts described in great detail the manner in which the negotiations were carried out, and commented on the powerful memory that the local tribesmen had; however, he pointed out that during the actual discussions of treaty terms, each native American held a different shell in his hand as each article was discussed.

"After the conclusion of the matter," wrote Danckaerts, "all the children who have the ability to understand and remember it are called together, and then they are told by their fathers, sachems, or chiefs how they entered into such a contract with these parties." The children were shown the shells and asked to "plant each one in particular to their memory." These young people were told how important it was for them to remember all this data, so as not to break any treaties. The chief then bound the shells together on a string, put them in a bag, and kept it in his home with other items bound up with tribal history.

String figures were used by the peoples of the Pacific Islands to illustrate and help remember their myths and some historical tales. But even more intriguing is the fact that in the South Pacific, among the aboriginals of Australia, and in the northernmost areas of the Pacific, among Eskimo peoples, there is a pictorial form of storytelling shared principally by women and girls. The aboriginal Australians draw in the sand, using a finger; the Eskimo draw in the snow or mud, using a storyknife.

These storyknives were made of whalebone and were beautifully crafted and decorated. Fathers or older brothers made them for the girls in a family, and their sole function was for the pleasurable custom of drawing the stories girls told each other for entertainment.

Another country in which children (of both sexes) love to make pictures while they tell short stories is Japan. Wherever one goes throughout the country, in playgrounds, parks, gardens, or in front of private homes, at certain seasons one will always find a group of children entertaining each other with clever or funny sketches, accompanied by chanted tales of sense or nonsense. Two examples of these are given in my book *The Story Vine*.

These are but a few examples of the use of pictures or three-dimensional objects to remember crucial periods of tribal history, important myths, moral lessons, or simply entertaining fictions.

Present-day families often don't realize it, but they, too, have objects associated with a family story. Photographs in old albums, jewelry or ornaments associated with ancestors or some momentous occasion, household utensils carried by immigrant families over long distances, quilts made of discarded clothing that once combined beauty and utility— any one of these could be the source of story.

PART FOUR

How to Tell Stories

Telling stories in a family setting should be less demanding than telling them in a public or professional situation. The key quality to aim for is a naturalness that makes it appear as though the story were just rolling out of your imagination. This is not as easy as it sounds.

We are all losing the verbal facility that used to come as part of general education. This is due partly to the fact that we now rely greatly on visual media for acquiring information and partly because education today gives less emphasis to rhetoric. We get much less of a chance to practice our literature-speaking voices than we did only a few decades ago. We are hardly ever asked to train our memories, in the belief that machines can do it better. Even the books we do read have been shortened, cut in vocabulary, and simplified.

Reading aloud from good printed versions of myths, folk and fairy tales, and other great story literature can help to rebuild the imagery, vocabulary, and structure necessary to tell a story well. Some of our modern writers also have styles that tease the tongue and beg to be spoken aloud. However, as one of those writers, Jane Yolen, has said: "The eye and the ear are different listeners." In her book *Touch Magic*, she writes:

> What sounds well at night by a listening child's bed does not read as well on the page. What lies perfectly formed in Bodoni Bold [type] on the white sheet may stutter on the tongue tomorrow. I could never write down and make a book of stories of the absurd "Silly Gorilly" which entertained my three children through years of bed-

time telling. How can I recapture my own lumbering gallop around the room, the infection of giggles shared, the pauses, the tickles, the rolling of eyes? On the other hand, how does one deal with sight rhymes like rain/again or wind/kind, rhymes that resonate to the eye but do not work well on the twentieth-century American tongue?

This description captures very well the intimate hilarity one can try for when telling stories to very young children. During that period, the parent or adult must often "pull out all the stops" to keep the attention of egocentric toddlers. Also, the sense of humor of the young child focuses a great deal on the ridiculous and the nonsensical.

Some parents keep this exaggerated style even when telling stories to older children. They gesticulate wildly, change voices to suit each character, pantomime much of the action, or make their faces contort in every possible way. The children continue to find this amusing because it reminds them of the many funny moments they have shared like this before.

Such a style is not very subtle, but it is perfectly suited to many of the very repetitious tales that young children like; or to the made-up stories in which they are characters; or the tricky stories that involve string or paper or a handkerchief.

Those parents who feel inhibited and can't see themselves carrying on to such a degree over a silly story should see to it that their children do get at least some of this kind of nonsense, if they seem to like it and want it. Perhaps a baby-sitter can be chosen precisely because he or she has this facility. Nonsense complements sense, and most young children need a generous dose of it.

But there comes the moment when the storyteller wants something more than giggles in the way of response. And the child listener is also waiting for the person who can make the telling of even a simple story a high art, with the full power of dramatic catharsis. Frances Clarke Sayers, a librarian and critic of children's books, remembered vividly the moment she first heard a story told "with style and formality," so that it was lifted beyond the realm of casual family storytelling.

She writes:

For me, the memory goes back to a year when I was the only child in a household of maiden aunts, a grandmother, and a young and handsome bachelor uncle.

Often, on Sundays, there would be young lady guests for dinner, and though I was "too young to know," I sensed that my uncle, like the prince in Andersen's story, was "inspecting a number of princesses." I always felt sorry for those young women who came, one by one, because so many pairs of eyes were upon them.

I had no patience with my uncle, either, for the choice was perfectly clear in my mind. I cannot recall her name, but her eyes were brown, her hair the exact shade of her eyes; she was short and plump, and I would know her voice were I even to hear it in paradise. She told me "The Gingerbread Boy," I sitting, not in her lap, but on a stool at her feet. She told it as though she were relating a tale as great in magnitude as *Hamlet*, as indeed it was to me, because it was to her. It was mystery, and tragedy, and delight, and in all the subsequent years of telling tales and listening, I have never dared to tell it myself, nor have I ever heard it told as well.

That woman who told the story to Mrs. Sayers was not a professional actress but a kindergarten teacher. She had probably learned, through trial and error, some of these basic lessons:

1. To tell a story with intensity and conviction does not necessarily mean telling with exaggeration.
2. A soft, natural voice sometimes speaks in greater volume than a shout or screech.
3. The hint of a gesture can be more mysterious and suggestive than the outright pantomiming of an action.
4. Timing is very important; if even a few words are spoken too quickly or too slowly, the basic thrust of the story will not come through.
5. Telling stories to young children or other persons who are smaller, younger, or simply seated lower than the storyteller should not give the teller license to talk down to the listeners.
6. Likewise, the storyteller should not force her- or himself, simply

for effect, to reach beyond a range of storytelling that is comfortable.

7. There is nothing more effective than stories told by tellers who love their tales and know them well.

That kindergarten teacher may have learned to tell stories beautifully because she read many folk and fairy tales over and over, year in and year out, always watching the responses of the children and interacting with them. As mentioned before, this is one of the best ways of learning story-telling. The language of these tales, if one selects a well-told version, is smooth and effortless. After reading one over and over again, you may be surprised to find that whole paragraphs surface in your memory, often triggered by a key word or image.

Sometimes selecting four or five different versions of the same story and reading them aloud can be just as helpful. There are countless ways of saying the same thing, and by comparing the ways in which several tellers or writers or translators have interpreted a fairy tale, we often find that it becomes a new story for us.

Most adults do not have a great deal of time to study a lot of stories and then explore the meanings behind them and how best to tell them. They must start by using the emotional responses they already have experienced with stories from the past—either stories they have lived or those they have read or heard.

A good way to begin is with some event from childhood or youth that still brings a rush of deep feeling each time you think of it. Try to run this event through your imagination slowly, as though you were projecting a film at slow speed. Do this several times, and then begin to put phrases and sentences to some of your mind pictures. See if you can find the phrase or sentence that expresses exactly what you feel when each of the key images pop up in your head.

Tell the story of this event to someone with whom you feel comfort-able. At this stage, don't worry about getting all the phrases right. But do consciously tell it as a story, and try to use as many complete phrases and sentences (and as few *uh*s and *you know*s) as possible. Always keep in mind those inner pictures, rolling as smoothly as a film.

Later, try to remember what you left out, and see if you can figure out why. This might give you a clue to a picture or word you must bring to mind in order to remember that particular part of the story. Tell your story again to a different person, and see if you do any better. Keep telling it, usually to one person at a time, until you have told it at least six times.

Then, test yourself by asking yourself whether you truly feel you have improved the quality and ease of your telling. Try, in retrospect, to examine the responses of your listeners. Did they seem to come away from their hearing of the story with some of the same emotions that you felt in recalling it? Did they show different emotions? Or did they seem merely polite in their attention?

The personal experience story, used in this way, can often be the best practice for developing skill in telling all types of story. Sometimes, the first telling strikes a resonance in you and your listener(s) that seems just right. Then, you try it again, and you get a different response. This generally gives you an indication that you still have more in the story to explore. However, such stories can be tried out fairly easily, because in most social situations, one has the opportunity to tell such a story.

Hearing other storytellers is another method to use in becoming a storyteller, because it gives clues as to what you might do at certain points in specific stories. Or it may show you that certain habits of gesturing or pantomiming are distracting and take away from the story, so that you want to stop using them.

Almost every community in North America has storytelling events, either for children or for adults or both. Find out about such programs in your community (see page 143) and attend as many as you can. Whether or not you use the techniques you see in such sessions, you will probably learn something useful to you in your family storytelling. But, most importantly, you will probably have an enjoyable time.

If you can follow these three basic rules, you will be able to tell at least a few family stories, and tell them well:

1. Be natural.
2. Don't exaggerate unless the natural purpose of the story is silly or nonsensical entertainment.
3. Believe in the story you are telling, either literally or symbolically or both.

PART FIVE

Some Easy and Entertaining Stories to Tell

Stories for the Very Young

As mentioned before in the section on bedtime, the first stories to use with young children are nursery rhyme stories. If you cannot remember them well, refresh your memory by reading them aloud from books at first. However, do try to use at least some of them in a purely oral style, since that is how they were originally passed on. Also, it will add to your enjoyment not to have the book come between you and the child.

The next stage can be the reading aloud of very simple picture books with only a brief story line. You can find a wide selection in your local public library and in bookstores that specialize in children's books. Try out a variety of these and observe your children's responses.

After that, try to make up stories spontaneously. Use themes from books that the child has liked, or events that have happened to the child or to you. Put your child or children in the stories by name, if they seem to like that.

A few examples of such stories have already been given in earlier sections. Here is another example, a story I have used since my days as a children's librarian in New York, some thirty years ago. Age three or four seems to be the time when children like it most. You can tell it as given here or adapt it in a way that suits you and your listeners. For instance, you can call the central character Michael, as in the original picture book, or you can use the name of one of the children in your audience. If you do not wish to tell all of the episodes, select one or two, perhaps after seeing your child act out something. Add episodes based on your own observations of the way children pretend to be animals or objects. Keep in mind that children between the ages of two and five like this combination of ordinary, everyday realism and escapism. Make up other stories using the same concepts.

MAGIC MARY

This story was inspired by the book Magic Michael *by Louis Slobodkin, published by Macmillan in 1944. The humorous yet not cartoonist illustrations are in the inimitable Slobodkin style. The original text is in free rhyme, sometimes rather forced, and not all the pretend activities are particularly childlike. One suspects they were chosen to give good subjects for the illustrator's fancy. Gradually, through many retellings, I have changed and expanded the things the child character pretends to be or to do, and I use a girl as often as a boy as that central character. I use rhyme and repetition for the key phrases, but this is not necessary to make the story effective. Some children want to know what the "magic" is, in which case the teller can talk about the "magic" in imagination. Other children do not require this to be spelled out for them.*

There was once a girl named Mary who was not happy just being an ordinary girl. She was always wanting to be something else. Something fierce and powerful or tiny and mischievous. Luckily for her, she had some magic that let her be almost anything.

One day Mary's older brother came home from grocery shopping. He had bought food for his camping trip that weekend. Most of the things he left in the big brown bag, but the string cheese he put in the refrigerator.

"Don't you touch it!" he warned his sister, because he knew how much Mary loved string cheese. She liked to pull off thin strips and suck them slowly into her mouth, chewing as she went. It was almost as much fun as eating spaghetti.

As soon as her brother left the kitchen, Mary began to get quieter and quieter.

> She sat without moving;
> Stillness filled the house.
> Mary was using her magic;
> She was a little mouse.

And that mouse opened the refrigerator and was taking a nibble of the string cheese, when suddenly Mary's brother came into the room.

"Leave my cheese alone, you little mouse!" he scolded.

So Mary went off to play with her toys. She lined up all the miniature cars she owned. Behind them she lined up the cars that belonged to her brother and that he hardly played with anymore. She gave the last car in line a push, but it would not move. It was too small to push all the cars in front. So Mary got a string and connected all the cars together. Then she got in front of all of them, took hold of the string, and started off.

"*Brrrm. Brrrm. Brrrm.*"

> The line started moving;
> The cars were not stuck;
> Mary was using her magic;
> She was a big towing truck.

The towing truck pulled the line of cars into the hall, past the kitchen, and through the living room. "*Brrrm. Brrrm. Brrrm!*"

"Must you make so much noise, Miss Tow Truck?" asked Mary's mother. So Mary unhitched all the cars and took them back to the play-room.

That afternoon, Mary put on her dancing slippers. She danced all over the living room rug. Just then the door opened and in walked her uncle. He was stopping by to say hello. He reached out his arms to give Mary a hug. *ZZZZT!* As soon as he touched Mary, a spark crackled in the air. Mary opened her eyes wide and then she laughed. She danced again, rubbing her shoes over the rug, and then touched her uncle. *ZZZZT!* Another spark flew off her fingers. Again and again she danced, sliding her shoes over the rug, and every few minutes she would stretch out one hand to touch her uncle.

> She twisted and turned and slid
> Like the flames in a leaping fire;
> Mary was using her magic
> To become an electric live wire.

Mary's uncle grabbed hold of her. "So, Miss Live Wire, you're full of electricity, is that it?" he asked. "Well, if you have so much electricity in you, then any hairs you have must be standing on end." And Mary's uncle picked up that live wire and tipped it upside down, until all its hairs were standing on end, just like this! (You might like to pick up a child listener and turn her upside down.)

On Sunday in May, Mary and her family went for a jog in the zoo. There were baby animals everywhere. They jogged past baby bears sleeping curled up next to their mothers and past monkey babies clinging to the hair on their mothers' backs. They stopped jogging to watch the baby kangaroos peeping out of their mothers' pockets.

When they got home, Mary's mother said, "Take off your jogging suit and put on something nice. Grandma is coming to dinner, and you know how she likes to see you in one of the pretty dresses she gave you."

But Mary did not hear her mother. She was hopping from the front door to her room. She took a brown furry animal from her bed and stuffed it down the front of her pants! It made a big bulge—right here! The head stuck out over the elastic of her waistband. She hopped all the way back to the living room, just as Grandma was coming in the door.

> Grandma at once saw the situation;
> No need to ask: "What are you?"
> Mary was using her magic.
> Now she was a kangaroo!

"Well, Mrs. Kangaroo, can't you stop jumping around so that I can give you a kiss?" asked Grandma. The kangaroo stopped long enough for a kiss and then hopped on.

The following Saturday Mary did wear a dress. It was her birthday and she was getting ready for her party. She wore the best dress she had, with a wide, whirly-twirly skirt. As soon as she had put it on, she began to turn in circles.

> Mary kept twirling and whirling;
> It looked like she'd never stop.
> Mary was using her magic;
> She was a spinning top.

At that moment Mary's father came home, pushing a huge box.

"My word, where did that spinning top come from?" asked Father. He opened one end of the box, and the spinning top slowed down enough to see a big red wheel. Father opened the other end, showing another big wheel, and the top slowed down some more. Father opened the cover of the box, and out popped a pair of handlebars.

"Too bad," he said. "Too bad we only have tops and boys around this house. This isn't a bike for tops or boys."

> Now there was no more spinning;
> Now there was no more whirl.
> Mary stopped using her magic.
> She said: "Of course, I'm a girl."

And as soon as her party was over, do you know how Mary used her magic? (You can leave this open-ended and imply that the child listeners should supply the answer, or you can give whatever answer you feel appropriate to the situation, e.g., "She used her magic to be an acrobat so she wouldn't fall off her bike.")

WHO LIVES IN THIS LITTLE HOUSE?
A Folk Tale to Tell on the Fingers

I have adapted this from the version found in *Old Peter's Russian Tales* by Arthur Ransome. Some versions change the skull to a box or a mitten, and I suspect this is due to the squeamishness of the teller. Make that change if you prefer. However, I think the skull adds just the right touch of mystery. This story was the perfect answer for me when, on a walk through the woods with a small grandnephew, we came upon just such a skull, picked clean and lying there. He was a bit scared, but after I answered his questions and told this story, ending with the bear hug, he could bring himself to touch the skull with a finger and get rid of his fear.

Once upon a time, the skull of an animal lay on the open plain.

Take one of child's hands and make it into curved, tentlike shape, by curving your hand over it.

The skull was just empty bone. It had been picked clean by the ants, and it shone white in the sunshine.

Take little finger of child's other hand. Hold it up while you hold the other fingers and thumb flat in the child's palm.

Burrowing Mouse came along, twitching his whiskers and looking around at the world. He saw the skull and thought it looked like a fine place to live. He stood up in front of the house and called out:

"Little house, little house! Who lives in this little house?"

No one answered, for there was no one inside.

"I will live there myself," said Burrowing Mouse. In he went, and he set up house in the skull.

Croaking Frog came along, jump, jump, jump.

"Little house, little house," croaked Frog. "Who lives in this little house?"

"I am Burrowing Mouse. I live in this little house. Who are you?"

"I am Croaking Frog. I would like to live in that house, too."

"Come in and make yourself at home," said Burrowing Mouse.

So Croaking Frog went in, and they began to live together happily, the two of them.

Then Rabbit Run-and-Hide came hopping by.

Poke child's little finger into the cupped hand and wiggle it a bit. Then bring it out and tuck it down with other fingers.

Take ring finger of child's uncupped hand. Hold it up while holding down the other fingers in child's palm.

Poke little finger of child's other hand through hole made by thumb and fingers in cupped hand. Wiggle it as mouse answers:

Pull out little finger. Flatten it in palm. Hold up ring finger.

Flatten ring finger, poke little finger through hole in cupped hand.

Poke little finger and ring finger into cupped hand and wiggle. Then bring out both and flatten against palm.

Hold up child's middle finger while holding others flat.

"Little house, little house! Who lives in this little house?" asked Rabbit Run-and-Hide.

"Burrowing Mouse and Croaking Frog. We live in this little house. Who are you and what do you want?"

"I am Rabbit Run-and-Hide. I want to hide in the little house and live there, too."

"Well, come along in. We have room for you, too," said Croaking Frog and Burrowing Mouse.

"Here I come, then," said Rabbit Run-and-Hide, as he flattened his ears and hopped into the house. They began to live together nicely, the three of them: Burrowing Mouse, Croaking Frog, and Rabbit Run-and-Hide.

Then Fox Fleet-and-Fast came running by. He looked at the skull and called out: "Little house, little house! Who lives in this little house?"

"Burrowing Mouse and Croaking Frog and Rabbit Run-and-Hide. We live in this house. And who are you?"

"I am Fox Fleet-and-Fast. I would like to share this little house."

"Come on in. We have room for you," said Burrowing Mouse, Croaking Frog, and Rabbit Run-and-Hide.

Flatten middle finger. Poke little finger and ring finger through hole in cupped hand.

Pull out little and ring fingers and flatten. Hold up middle finger.

Flatten middle finger. Poke little and ring fingers through hole in cupped hand.

Pull out two fingers. Hold up middle finger.

Poke middle finger into cupped hand. Pull out and flatten. Hold up index finger.

Flatten index finger. Poke little, ring, and middle fingers through hole in cupped hand.

Pull out three fingers. Flatten. Hold up index finger.

Flatten index finger. Poke three fingers in hole again.

Pull out three fingers. Hold up index finger, poke it into cupped hand, wiggle, pull out again. Then flatten it and hold up thumb.

The four animals lived together for a time, when along came Wolf Wily-and-Wise. He saw the skull, walked up to it, and called out: "Little house, little house! Who is living in this little house?"

Flatten thumb. Poke four fingers into hole.

"We are Burrowing Mouse, Croaking Frog, Rabbit Run-and-Hide, and Fox Fleet-and-Fast. We live in this house. And who are you?"

Pull out four fingers. Flatten. Hold up thumb.

"I am Wolf Wily-and-Wise. I would like to live in that little house with you."

Flatten thumb. Poke four fingers through hole.

"Come in, then," said Burrowing Mouse, Croaking Frog, Rabbit Run-and-Hide, and Fox Fleet-and-Fast. "We have room for you."

Pull out four fingers. Hold up thumb.

Wolf Wily-and-Wise had to push hard to get in, but he did, and the five animals lived together in that little house.

Push thumb into cupped hand. Then take out and make fist of child's uncupped hand.

Along came Bear Big-and-Brown. He was very slow and heavy. He lumbered up to the skull and called out: "Little house, little house! Who lives in this little house?"

Poke five fingertips through hole in cupped hand.

"We do. We are Burrowing Mouse, Croaking Frog, Rabbit Run-and-Hide, Fox Fleet-and-Fast, and Wolf Wily-and-Wise."

Pull out fingertips. Make fist again.

"I am Bear Big-and-Brown and I've come along to squash you all with a big bear hug!"

Adult teller squeezes both of child's hands and then gives child a big hug.

Handkerchief Stories

Some twenty years ago, I heard and saw my first handkerchief story. It used the mouse figure, described below, and was told by a grandparent to two grandchildren in a home in Germany. At the time I thought it was a trick developed by that person on his own, and was not aware that this entire genre of handkerchief tricks and stories had existed for some years and had been passed on from one generation to the next, without ever being written down.

Later, after I had seen handkerchiefs used for showing tricks and telling short tales among a number of families in the United States, I began to be aware that in most cases, it was a grandparent of German, or Dutch, or Danish ancestry who had been the source of the clever stories. Usually, they had been learned in the early years in this century. Curiously, I also saw the mouse figure performed in Japan.

I searched and searched in folklore journals, books, and indexes for references to this type of tale, but I could not find a single reference.

On a trip to the Netherlands in February and March 1985, I spoke to several groups of librarians, teachers, and others working with children. I happened to mention that I was trying to locate folk references to family storytelling with handkerchiefs, and quite a number of persons in the audiences volunteered information about this kind of storytelling. All agreed they had never read anything about it, but simply remembered it from their childhood.

In Eindhoven, I stayed with Cecile Beijk van Daal and her family, and found a treasure trove of handkerchief stories. Most of the figures and stories given here I learned from her, or from family members and friends whom she brought in to help her remember what she had not attempted for several decades. I did find a few descriptions of them in books. However, none of the printed sources gave any indication of the earliest known use of the handkerchief in storytelling, or where it occurred.

THE PROFESSOR

Material needed: one handkerchief, any size. This story was remembered by many adults in my audiences, although it usually took some effort before they could recall the entire rhyme. I give it first in Dutch and then in English translation

Als heel de wereld stokvis was,
en elke boom een gas,
als zee en meer en waterplas,
eens louter haring was—
Waarmee lesten wij dan onze dorst?
Over dit gewichtig vraagstuk
hebben zeven professoren
zich zeven dagen lang
zitten te krabben achter hun oren.

If the whole world of dried fish was,
and every tree a gas,
if sea and lake and creek,
of only salted herring was—
With what could we quench our thirst?
About this important problem
seven professors have spent
seven long days
scratching behind their ears.

Take a corner of the handkerchief and make a knot in it; leave about 1 inch of the corner tip sticking up over the knot.

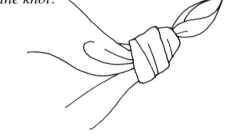

Place the tip of the index finger inside the handkerchief, under the knot. While reciting the first lines, have the "professor" slowly nod his head.

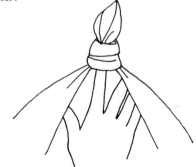

At the final line, reach up with thumb and scratch behind knot.

THE PEASANT AND HIS PLOT

Material needed: 5 handkerchiefs, approximately the same size

There was once a peasant who had a square plot of land. It was set in a large field owned by the lord of the manor. Here is his plot.

Lay out one handkerchief flat. (I like to lay it on a green tablecloth.)

At each corner of the peasant's plot there grew a tree. Here are the trees. All around the plot was green meadow or bushy fields.

The peasant married and after several years he had a family of five children. He looked around his plot and saw all of the empty fields not being used.

He went to the lord of the manor and said: "I need a bigger plot to grow enough food to feed my family."

Make a knot in each corner.

The lord of the manor said: "Very well, you may have a larger plot. I will allow you to add as much land as you wish, but only under these conditions:

1. Your plot must keep its square shape.
2. The trees must stay where they are.
3. The trees must remain at the edge of your plot.

Point to square shape of handkerchief. Point to four trees. Run your finger along edges.

When the peasant returned home, his wife asked: "Did he give us a bigger plot?" "He might as well have told us we cannot have a larger plot," said the peasant, as he repeated what the lord had stated. He laid out his handkerchief to show them what the conditions were.

1. The plot must stay square.
2. The trees must remain where they are.
3. The trees must be at the edge of our plot.

Repeat as above.

The peasant's wife shook her head; but his oldest daughter, who was a very clever girl, looked carefully at the problem and said: "Father, I will show you how to double the amount of land we have in our plot."

She ran and got four handkerchiefs, folded them carefully, and placed them like this.

"Well, if you aren't the clever one!" exclaimed her father. He saw that she had found a way to make the plot twice as big as it had been before. Yet it was still square, the trees would be in the same places, and they would still be at the edge of the new plot.

"I am such a stupid fellow," said her father. "I would never have found such an answer. How did you think of it?"

"You are not stupid, Father," answered the girl. "You sent me to school, and there I learned to read. I found this answer in a book."

So the peasant doubled his land, thanks to his clever daughter and the fact that she had learned to read.

Fold the remaining four handkerchiefs into triangles. Place them along the four sides of the spread-out handkerchief, as shown in diagram.

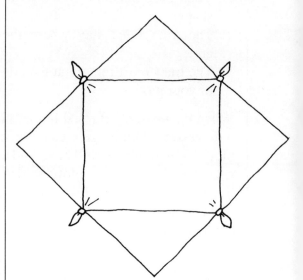

RABBIT STORY

Materials needed: 1 large white handkerchief or napkin. One of the Dutch librarians told me that as a child he would often refuse to eat everything on his plate. His grandfather would say "Too bad! Then I can't tell you about the rabbit." Only after the food was gone from his plate did his grandfather consent to take the white dinner napkin and make the rabbit, and tell rabbit stories. Others reported to me that it was a story designed to remind them always to have a clean handkerchief in their pockets, in the days before Kleenex! I have combined both ideas here, and give the opening to what could be a whole series of short rabbit stories, limited only by the adult's imagination.

This is a small hill, with a peaked point at its top.	*Fold the handkerchief in half.*
	Fold the bottom over, approximately 1 inch. Fold over again 1 inch, and a third time 1 inch. Do this as you mention digging away the earth.
If you were to shovel away the earth at the bottom of the hill,	
	You will end up with Figure C. Quickly fold it over sideways, at the midpoint, and then flip the entire figure so that the hill point is upside-down.
you would find, deep down inside, a snug little den.	*The hill point now becomes the rabbit's den. Snuggle a finger or two in the folds of the "den" when referring to it.*

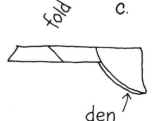

In that den lived a
soft
white
cuddly
rabbit.

He had a twitching nose
and two long ears. Well,
one day, the rabbit came
out of his den and hopped
along the road. The first
person he met was a little
(boy/girl) wearing a
(describe dress, jacket,
jeans, or whatever child
is wearing that has a
pocket). The (girl/boy)
picked up the rabbit and
stroked it. And then,
whish! (she/he) popped
the rabbit into (her/his)
pocket. And do you
know, the rabbit liked it
so much in that pocket,
he wasn't sure he ever
wanted to go home to his
den at the bottom of the
hill.

*While saying these
words, grasp the figure
in your hands as shown;
the thumb holds down
the two ends; the hill
point (den) is held
loosely in the back by
little and ring fingers.*

*Bring the hill point (den)
up, around, and through
the hole where your
index and middle
fingers were.*

*Tighten the knot and
shape into a rabbit's
head.*

Open out the two ears.

*Make rabbit hop along
edge of table.*

Stroke rabbit.

*Pop rabbit into child's
pocket.*

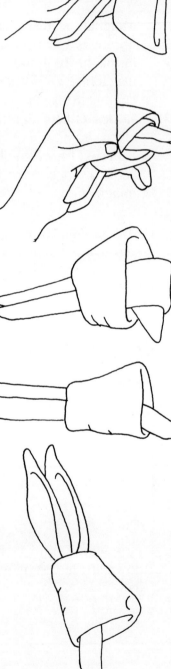

MOUSE STORY

Materials needed: 1 large white handkerchief. This figure is very old. It is the only one that can be found mentioned in some of the early books on the history of the handkerchief. I have encountered it in a number of families in the United States and Europe, and once in Japan. I have also seen it used by religious ministers to enliven Sunday School classes for the very young. This was recalled by at least ten of the Dutch librarians. Most often, there was no specific story mentioned; rather, the person remembering how it had been used by a parent or grandparent could only recall vague bits and pieces of stories. Obviously, each person invented stories to suit the situation, or perhaps played with the mouse only as a game. My story is made up to show how I might use the mouse figure, but the best way to tell a "Mouse Story" is to compose your own, to fit your own sense of humor and that of the child or children listening to you. To achieve the jumping action of the mouse, which is mentioned by most of those persons who had enjoyed this activity as children, it is essential to practice with the mouse figure. If you are wearing a long-sleeved suit when you tell the story, the mouse will sometimes cling nicely to it. Experiment and see what you can and cannot make the mouse do.

One night, I came downstairs in the dark and saw that there was something moving on the table. I threw my handkerchief down to see if I could catch it.

Spread handkerchief flat on table.

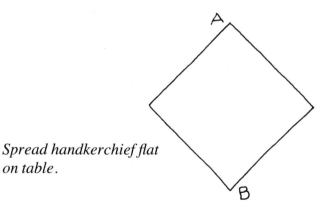

The thing wiggled some more, so I thought I would try to wrap my handkerchief around it. I folded over the two ends and then I wound the handkerchief around and around. All the while, I could feel that thing wiggling and squirming inside.

Fold it into triangle. Fold over each of the two side points, so that they meet in the middle and are even at the bottom. Now roll up, making at least three or four complete turns. Roll up to about 4 inches below Points A and B.

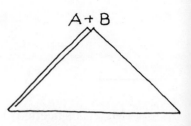

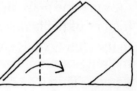

Turn entire figure over.

Fold over each of the two rolled sides so they overlap about 1 inch.

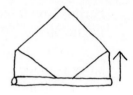

It went from one side to the other.

Roll up half turn.

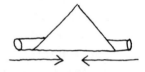

Tuck Points A and B into pocket where the 2 rolled sides are nesting tightly against each other. Make sure the points are tucked in above the folded rolls.

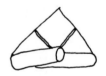

I put my fingers inside for a moment. I could feel something.

Place your thumbs into pocket on side of figure opposite to where you tucked in Points A and B. Place your index fingers behind the ends of figure and your other fingers underneath.

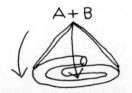

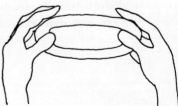

I tried turning my hand-
kerchief inside out; nothing there.

I did it again. Still nothing.

I flipped it over again and
this time I could see
something. So I carefully
opened one end and tried
to grab hold of it. But that
wiggly thing moved to
the other side. I opened
up the other end, and just
then I could feel that
thing trying to squeeze
out, so I tied up the end as
fast as I could.

*Turn figure inside out, in
much the same way you
would turn a small bag
inside out.*

*You will end up with
another pocket facing
you. Put your thumbs in
it, and again turn figure
inside out.*

Repeat a third time.

*You will now see the
Points A and B reappear,
but they will be partly
tucked underneath the
upper layer of the figure,
one on each end.*

*Carefully pull out the
shorter point, usually on
the left. This will be the
mouse's tail.*

*Pull out the larger point,
usually on the right.
Spread it, as shown,
allowing the tip of point
to tuck under. Then tie
these two sides into a
knot. This is a bit tricky,
but practice helps. The
knot makes the head and
the two side tips make
the ears of the mouse.*

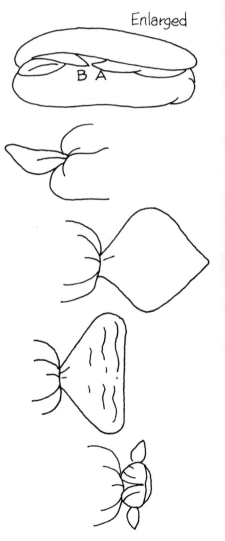

Enlarged

But I wasn't fast enough because there sat a little white mouse, staring at me. Suddenly, he jumped up my arm! I pounced on him to catch him again and put him back in my hand. He jumped higher up my arm! I was determined not to let that mouse get away, so I pounced again, but this time the mouse leaped higher than ever. He jumped so high that he landed right in the lap of

a little (girl/boy) who was sitting there. And at first they both got scared—the mouse and the little (girl/boy). But after a bit they were not frightened of each other at all.

Figure is now complete.

Hold mouse in palm of hand, head up. The tips of the fingers should be curved lightly right below mouse's tail.

Stroke the mouse and when you are ready to make it jump, flip the fingertips quickly upward. You will have to practice the amount of pressure needed to get the mouse to jump up, then jump higher, and finally, jump off your arm into the child's arms or lap.

DOLL BABIES, OR BABIES IN THE CRADLE

Materials needed: 1 handkerchief, any size. Cecile's daughter, now a university graduate, came in as we were making handkerchief figures; she reminded her mother how much she used to love it, when she had been sick and was starting to feel better, to have handkerchief babies spread all over the bed. Cecile made the babies in many positions, simply by tying the knots in different ways.

Make a triangle out of hand-kerchief, bringing Point B up to Point A.

Tightly roll one side inward, almost up to center; pat down roll to hold it in place.

Repeat on other side.

While holding both rolls carefully with one hand, grasp Point B in your teeth. Grasp Point A with your other hand and bring it down and around the rolls.

Set figure down; arrange "babies" in the cradle, side by side, and swing it while singing "Rock-a-Bye-Babies." Drop cradle into child's lap at last line.

73

Origami (Paperfolding) Stories
by Gay Merrill Gross

While origami or paperfolding was practiced mainly by the Japanese for many hundreds of years, during the twentieth century it has become increasingly well known among people all over the world. The simplicity and delight of creating a decoration, a toy, or a useful object from only a sheet of paper has universal appeal.

My idea in creating these stories was to help the person learning how to make these models remember the sequence of folds by remembering the sequence of the story. After telling the stories to children, you might like to teach them how to do the folds.

If you wish to buy origami paper and cannot find it, send for a free source list from The Origami Center of America, 15 West 77th Street, New York, NY 10024.

SOMETHING SPECIAL

Materials needed: 1 sheet of origami paper, $5^1/2$ or $9^1/2$ inches square, blue on one side and white on the other. The swan is a traditional Japanese fold. The other folds are simply stages to get one to the final fold.

Once there was a cloud, drifting very slowly, ever so gently through the sky.

Hold square over your head in front of you, white side facing audience; slowly move paper to give idea of cloud drifting overhead.

Suddenly, the sky turned dark. You could hear the thunder cracking.

Large drops of rain started falling from the sky,

So much rain poured down that it filled a deep valley and formed a small lake.

Someone said to me: "If you go to that lake, you'll find something there that's very special. So I decided to go and see for myself.

At the edge of the lake was a lovely mountain, as perfectly shaped as Mount Fuji in Japan. "Is it the mountain that is so special here?" I asked some passersby.

"It is a wonderful mountain, especially if you climb to the top to look at the view," they replied. "But there's something else special at the lake."

Turn square so blue side faces audience. Make the paper crackle by pushing it slightly together and then pulling it apart.

Lower square as if drops of rain were falling.

Hold sheet flat in your hand, at waist level, with blue side up.

Turn paper so white side is facing up. Fold bottom corner up to top corner, making blue triangle.

Show triangle shape to represent mountain. At mention of climbing, run finger up one side to top of triangle; then run finger down other side.

Open paper back to blue square. Fold the two side edges to the center crease, as shown.

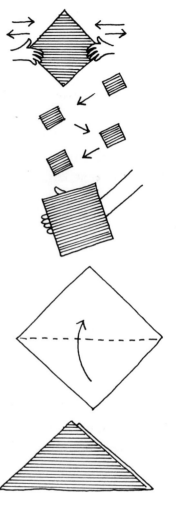

I walked until I came near a small restaurant at the foot of the mountain. A girl was coming out, licking on a big, blueberry ice cream cone.

Show blueberry ice cream cone. You might want to take an imaginary lick!

"Is that delicious? Is that the special thing here at the lake?" "It is delicious," answered the girl. "And special. But there is something else special here at the lake. Keep going and look all around you."

Open paper back to white square. Fold the two side edges to the center crease, as shown.

I looked to the left, to the right. Then I looked down, and up. There, floating in the sky above the lake was a lovely kite!

Show kite by pretending to fly it through the air.

"Is that what's special?" I asked the kite-flyer.

"I like my kite," said the kite-flyer. "But it is only made of paper and I can easily make another if it tears. There is something much more special here at the lake."

With blue kite side of paper up, fold each side to center crease, making a long, thin point.

76

I continued walking, looking down. In the path I saw something blue and silky. I picked it up. It was a necktie.

"Perhaps what's special about this lake is that one finds beautiful things," I said to a young man coming up. But he only looked relieved and said: "Oh, you found my necktie. Thank you very much." And he took it back.

I continued walking along the edge of the lake. Suddenly, I saw something dart through the grass at the edge of the lake. It was a—most unusual snake.

"This must be the special thing. I have never seen such a blue snake before." "No, the special thing is up ahead," said the man with the necktie as he walked along behind me.

Turn figure so thin point is downward and hold the necktie up under your chin.

Turn figure over, to back side of necktie. Fold in half, down the center crease, the long way.

With your hands, make the long, thin point wiggle like a snake.

Unfold center crease and turn so necktie figure is facing up.

I heard a "Rat-a-tap-tap-tap" coming from high in a tree at the edge of the lake. Looking up, I saw a woodpecker, tapping against the trunk of the tree.

But the woodpecker flew away, in the direction opposite from the lake. It couldn't be the woodpecker, if it didn't even live near the lake. I continued on my way. Suddenly, in the distance, I noted something gliding slowly across the water. As I came closer I could see it had a very small head and a long, graceful neck. It was a—swan.

The swan drifted slowly, gently through the water, just as the cloud had drifted, up in the sky.

Bring thin Point A up to fat Point B and press down well at the fold.

Fold thin point down a little to form a small head. The figure will begin to look like a bird.

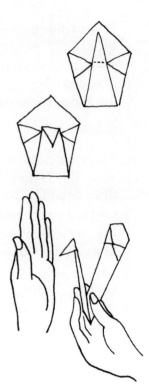

Grasp figure at fold and hold sideways so that beak is close to palm of opposite hand.

Tap the beak back and forth, quickly, against the palm of the other hand.

Fold model in half, bringing both sides of bird downward. Head should remain on top. Grasp at point indicated by dark circle; with other hand, lift head gently upward, to angle shown. Pinch back of head to make crease firm. Now, lift neck up and away from body. Pinch at base of neck to set crease. Move swan gracefully back and forth, and in turns.

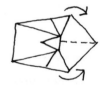

THE BROTHERS SHORT AND
THE BROTHERS LONG

Materials needed: 1 sheet of plain paper, 8¹/₂ by 11 inches, in any color. This story is based on a model known to paperfolders as "The Magazine Cover Box." If you separate the front and back covers from a magazine and use each sheet to fold a figure, you will have one for the box and one for its cover. This figure has been known for at least two hundred years in Europe and Asia. However, I do not use the paper from magazine covers since I do not want the pictures or text to distract from the story. Should you wish to make a cover for the box, start with a slightly larger sheet; otherwise you must crunch the box a bit in order for it to fit under the cover.

This is the story of the Brothers Short,	*Point to short edges of paper.*	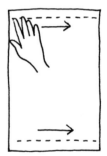
and the Brothers Long.	*Point out each long edge of paper.*	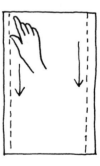

One day, the Brothers Long received a card.	*Fold paper in half, like a book, bringing long edges together.* *Show long card you have made.*
It was an invitation, and inside it said: "Meet at the center."	*Open card and point inside with your finger, as though you were reading a message.*
And so they did. One Brother Long went to the center.	*Open card; fold one long edge to center crease.*
The other Brother Long met him there. When they got there, the doors were open. So they went inside.	*Fold other long edge to center crease.* *Open out both flaps.*

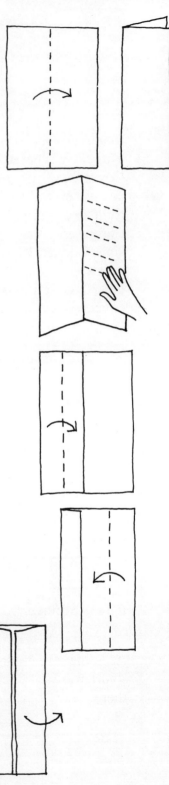

80

Now the Brothers Short, not to be left out,	*Rotate paper so short sides are now vertical; point to short sides again.*	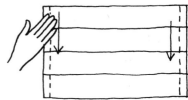
also received a card. It was also an invitation.	*Fold paper in half, bringing short sides of paper together.*	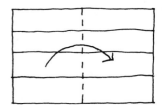
And inside this card it said: "Meet at the center." And so they did.	*Show card. Then open it and again point with your finger, as if reading a message.*	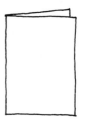 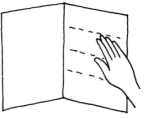
One Brother Short went to the center.	*Fold one short edge of paper to center crease. Hold up figure.*	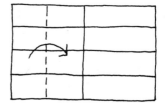
And the other Brother Short went to meet him there.	*Fold other short edge of paper to center crease.*	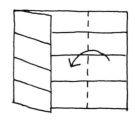

But when they got there —the doors were closed!

So they knocked and pushed very hard at the top of the left door.

Show figure. Make a fist and tap against one top corner, making a rustling sound as you strike paper.

They pushed so hard they made a dent in the top of that door. But the door still wouldn't open.

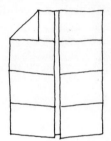

Bend in the corner and crease it, making sure you do not bend it so far in that you cannot later make the flaps. You might wish to mark the bending point lightly with pencil.

They banged at the top of the door on the opposite side.

Hold up figure. With the palm of your hand, push against the other top corner.

They banged so hard that the corner was forced in. But they still had no way to open the doors.

Bend down the other top corner, at about the same angle, and the same amount back.

They were very determined to get inside, so they did not give up. Next, they rammed themselves against one of the lower corners and heaved. It crushed inward.

Hold up figure. Poke several fingers at one of bottom corners. Then fold that corner in at approximately the same angle and distance as others.

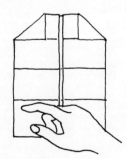

But the door would not open. This made them so angry they tried kicking the bottom on the other side. They kicked so hard they bent that corner inward as well. But the doors simply would not open. Now these brothers were very determined. They said to each other: "There must be some way to open these doors."

Then they noticed that there was a small crack right between the two doors. They said: "If we can make this opening just a little bigger, perhaps we can get inside." So they pushed the edge of one door back just a bit.

Hold up. Flick index finger off of thumb, hitting the other bottom corner with a snap.

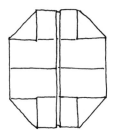

Fold in remaining bottom corner, same angle and distance as others.

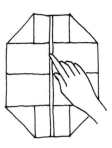

Show figure. Point to each folded-in corner. Point to slit where two doors meet.

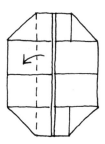

Fold one of short edges outward as far as you can, so it forms a flap that lies over turned-down corners.

Then they pushed the edge of the other door back. They were able to push it the same distance as the other door. Now they had a much larger opening between the two doors.

Instead of banging or kicking on the doors, they decided to push them very gently, gently. And the doors came apart.

And as they opened the doors, they saw a large sign hanging over the doorway. The sign said: Fill Me with Treasures.

When the Brothers looked down again, they saw a beautiful little box. It was a treasure box they had found behind the two doors. They gave it to me, and now I am giving the treasure box—to you!

Repeat on the other short edge of the figure.

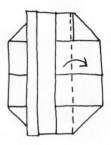

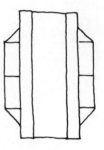

Slide your thumbs under the flaps and pull them up and apart; your paper will open up into a box.

As you are forming straight sides of box, and pinching them so they will stay in place, look up so as to divert attention. Be sure to curve sides of box inward a bit, to counteract their tendency to curve outward. Try to do this while reading the imaginary sign.

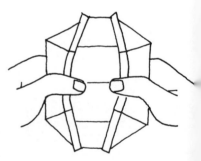

Show finished box.

Hand box to one of your listeners.

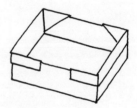

Paper Cutting or Tearing Stories

As in the case of handkerchief stories, I had seen a number of persons use paper cutting or tearing to accompany short stories that usually had a clever twist to them at the end. They have been almost impossible to trace in folklore journals or books, so I do not know their place of origin, or the approximate date they were first used. These stories seem to have special appeal to ministers and priests, because I have heard them most frequently from that group. In earlier decades, the tricks or deceptions behind the stories were almost certainly part of the repertoire of vaudeville entertainers and magicians. A number of professional handbooks for magicians, dating to the first two decades of this century, give instructions in how to do them.

Yet some of the tricks and tales almost surely predated this use by professional entertainers, because they are mentioned in books on paper and play that date to earlier centuries. Again, it is among the Dutch that one finds many playful examples of this kind of story.

THE APPLE THIEVES

Materials needed: Several old newspapers; 2 empty jam jars or tall mugs; a pair of scissors; 5 or 6 acorn "caps" are optional, if you can find them. Before beginning your story, prepare the newspaper in the following manner:

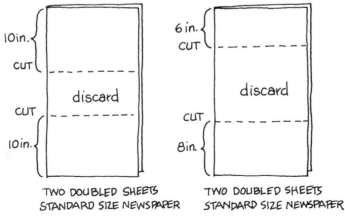

TWO DOUBLED SHEETS STANDARD SIZE NEWSPAPER   TWO DOUBLED SHEETS STANDARD SIZE NEWSPAPER

The four long 10-inch strips will be used for the trees, two for each tree. Prepare them in this way:

Roll one strip loosely, as though you were rolling it over a tube about 1½ inches in diameter. Just before you come to the end of the strip, lay the end of a second strip on top, so that about 2 inches overlap on each. Continue rolling until the second strip is all rolled up. Flatten one end and tuck it under a book or some other object. Now prepare the other two strips in the same manner and set that roll aside, next to the first one.

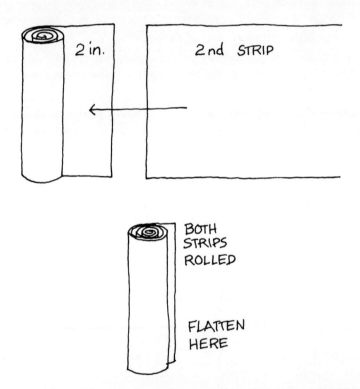

One of the 8-inch strips will be used for the fence. Prepare it thus: Fold it upward, the long way, in eight 1-inch pleats. That is, fold up 1 inch, turn strip over, fold up 1 inch, turn strip over, fold up 1 inch, turn strip over, etc. Make sure the folded edges are relatively even, each fold along the entire length of the fold. Press down on the folded edges just enough to keep them in place. Then, fold the accordion pleated strip in half, doubling its thickness and making it half as long.

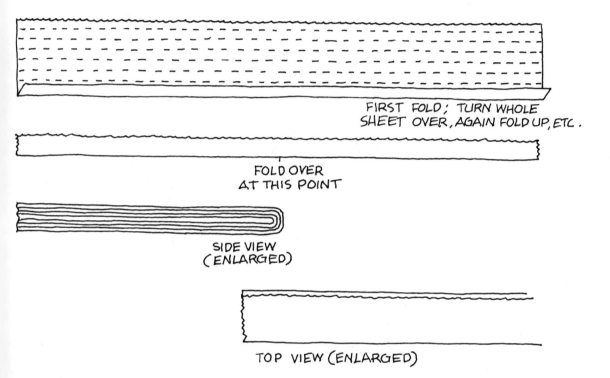

FIRST FOLD; TURN WHOLE SHEET OVER, AGAIN FOLD UP, ETC.

FOLD OVER AT THIS POINT

SIDE VIEW (ENLARGED)

TOP VIEW (ENLARGED)

Now, make cuts in the strip, first from one side, and then from the other. Try to cut as close to the edge as possible, without cutting the strip in half. You might have to do it several times, before you get a good example, because it is very easy for scissors to slip. When the cuts are made, leave the strip doubled up and put it aside.

Take the second 8-inch strip and roll it gently as though you were rolling it over a tube about 1 inch in diameter. Lightly flatten the center portion of the roll and set it aside by tucking it under a book or some other object that is handy. This will become the ladder.

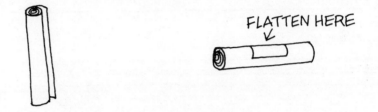

Now, take one of the 6-inch strips and fold it sideways into accordion pleats of about 2 inches. That is, fold sideways, turn over the strip, fold sideways, turn over, etc. You should get about fourteen folds. Lightly pencil in the outline figure of an elf on the outermost pleat. Make sure the middle of the elf is on the folded edge, as shown. Set this aside in some safe place.

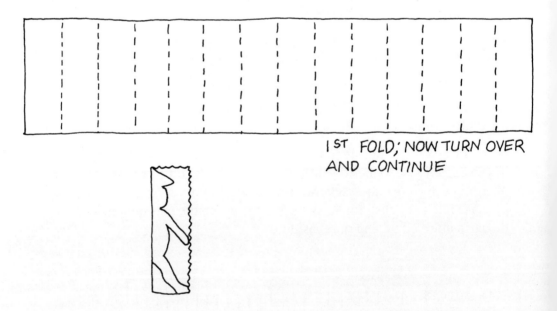

Now you are ready to begin the story. Have the scissors ready.

I had many flowers in my backyard but I did not have any trees. I decided I wanted to have some, so that I could have shade and fruit. Then one day, I got a seedling tree. I prepared a pot, planted the seedling tree in the pot, and watched it grow.

After a while, I decided the tree needed a friend, so I planted a second apple tree, in another pot that I had in my backyard. It grew and grew, just like the first one. But then they both stopped growing. And not a sign of an apple could I see. I wondered why I did not get any apples, but after I sat and watched my trees carefully for a few days, I knew why. The children were forever throwing their balls and breaking the branches; all the dogs in the neighborhood seemed to think the tree trunks were a gutter; and grown-ups would forget and lean something heavy agains the pots, knocking them over.

Take lightly flattened end of either of the two 10-inch rolls. Make four or five cuts through all thicknesses. The cuts should be about 6 inches down.

FLATTENED END

CUT

Set uncut bottom of roll in jam jar or mug. Pull up gently once or twice on the innermost layer of one of the cut strips. The tree will start to "grow." But do not pull too much.

Make second tree as above.

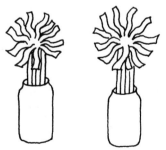

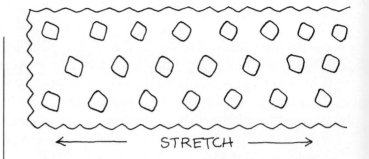

STRETCH

"I need a fence," I said to myself, and I quickly set about making one and placed it around my two apple trees.

The branches grew higher and filled out.

At last, they began to get tiny, green apples. The fruit got rounder and rosier every day.

Finally, I thought it was time to pick the apples from my two trees. I had no trouble reaching the lowest branches, but it seemed as though the reddest, plumpest fruit was in the highest branches.

"Now I need a ladder," I said to myself, so I decided to make one. I constructed a ladder as quickly as I could and set it up against one of the trees. However, by this time it was dark, so I decided to wait and pick my apples the following morning.

But the next day, when I came out to start picking fruit, I could see that more than half of the

PULL UP BRANCHES

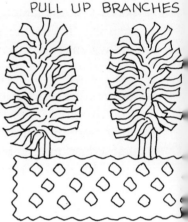

Take up fence strip and carefully open out. Stretch it around the two pots. Tuck one end in holes of the other end. It will hold sufficiently well for the duration of the story.

Take up 8-inch roll set aside for ladder. Flatten out roll gently and cut out upper part of center portion, as shown. Discard cut-out piece.

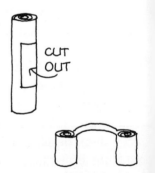

CUT OUT

Place the two side rolls in an up-and-down position, as shown. With your fingers, smooth out the center strip connecting them and push it up lightly from below, to get rid of crease. Now, pull up on the innermost papers of the side rolls. The ladder comes up and will reach to top of trees.

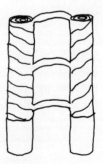

90

apples were gone. Someone had snuck into my backyard and stolen them. I wondered which of my neighbors it could be. I decided to stay up that night and watch from a secret hiding place, to see if the thief might return for the rest of those apples.

Just after midnight, I heard a soft singing. I peeked out from my hiding place and saw—not one of my neighbors but a troop of elves. They were dancing along and heading straight for my apple trees. They climbed or hopped inside the fence, and started to call out a magic chant. And the apples began to fall from the tree, one by one! I was so surprised that I let out a yell, and those elves just disappeared right before my eyes. I waited for the rest of the night, but they did not come back. But under my apple trees I found quite a few fallen apples and a ring of tiny, elfin hats.

Cut quickly around faint outline of elf you have penciled in on folded 6-inch strip.

Open up the elves strip and dance them over the trees.

Close up elves strip and whisk it out of sight.

Show the elfin acorn caps if you have them.

THE CAPTAIN FROM KRAKOW

Most of the figures in this story are quite old. As a paperfolding trick tale, the story of the sea captain is at least a hundred years old. However, I have changed it in a number of details. Because I tell this to two grandnephews and a grandniece, I choose to have three characters in the story. In order to put in a little about their Polish heritage, I make the young man come from Krakow and wear the typical square hat from that city, with its feather. However, you might wish to change this around to suit the child or children to whom you are telling. You can have the square hat as a university mortarboard, without the feather. You might want the captain to be a girl. There are also numerous other figures you can add to the story, should you have more children in your audience and want to give them each a part. In the books listed in Additional Sources of Good Stories to Tell (page 134), you can find folds to make a canoe, a catamaran, a Chinese junk, a rowboat, a fireman's hat, a baker's hat, a rain hat, and many others. Use this story only as a guide and invent your own variations.

Materials needed: sheets of newspaper, scissors, pencil, marking pen. Before you begin, you might want to have the following sheets of newspaper cut to size and in order, one on top of the other, for greater ease in telling, and less distraction to yourself and the audience. However, some children like getting involved in "helping" to prepare the paper for telling. You will have to be the judge as to which type are in your audience.

A double sheet refers to a full, double-spread page of newspaper, generally from 27 to 28 inches wide and 22 to 23 inches high. A single sheet is one-half that in size. In most cases you will use the sheet folded over, in the usual place where newspapers are folded. However, refold if necessary, to make sure the sides and bottom are even.

1 folded double sheet; cut bottom off so it is 18 inches high
2 strips each 14 inches long and 4½ inches wide, folded over
   to 7 by 4½
1 strip 23–28 inches long and 6–7 inches wide

1 folded double sheet; cut 3–4 inches off right sides, leaving
   20 inches
1 single sheet; cut approx. 9 inches off bottom, leaving a square
1 single sheet, folded down so each half is about 13½ by 11½
another of the same
still another of the same

There was once a young Polish man of Krakow who was not satisfied with his life.

Take up the folded double spread; place it in front of you with fold at top. Bring two upper corners down to middle, so they meet evenly. Press folds down.

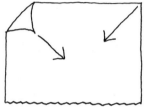

He had studied at the university but although he had learned much, he did not seem happy.

Fold up upper layer of bottom flap so it meets bottom edge of triangle. Then fold it up again so it covers bottom edge. Turn figure over.

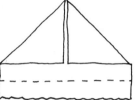

He sat around with his friends, drinking and playing cards and not doing much of anything.

Fold each side toward center so they meet. Then fold down top triangle and tuck it under the folded-over sides.

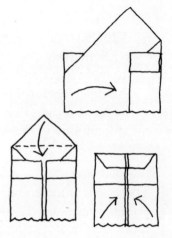

Fold in outer bottom corners so they meet in center. Fold up bottom point and tuck it behind band, but in front of folded-down upper triangle.

part side view

crown

bottom open apart

He always dressed in his best clothes when he went out.

Now, stand figure on its crown and gently press in on the two long sides, until two triangles appear. This will make the hat almost square. Crease it at equal points so it is four-cornered and square.

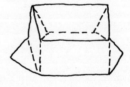

On his head he wore the four-cornered hat that all Krakow gentlemen wore in those days.

It looked a little like the hats our students wear when they graduate from school.

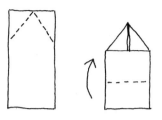

Turn figure over and set to one side. Take up one of the 7-by-4-inch strips and fold the outer corners of the folded edge so they meet in the middle, making triangle. Then fold up both layers of bottom edge so they just barely cover bottom edge of triangle. Now fold down the triangle. Press very hard on this last fold. Repeat the process for the second strip.

press hard on these folds

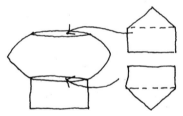

Take up main figure. Place flap of one folded strip behind band, with triangle pointing out. Place flap of other strip on opposite side, with triangle pointing out. Result will be a mortarboardlike hat.

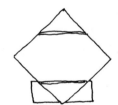

Roll 6-inch-wide strip over a pencil. Let pencil fall out; flatten one end of tube. Cut a slit down center of flattened end. Cut as many additional slits as possible.

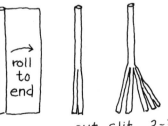

roll to end

cut slit 2-3 inches long

And, of course, to show that he was fashionable as well as clever, he always wore a peacock feather in one corner of his hat.

But the young man was bored. He liked the outdoor life and the wide open spaces. He went to ask his sister's advice. She was younger than he, but she was as clever and wise as a wizard. In fact, she was a wizard.

Sometimes, she wore the wizard hat that had been given to her by her great-grandmother. It was pointed and had stars embroidered all over it.

Pull up on center layer of cut strips, until you have a featherlike stalk. Tuck it in one corner of the hat. Put hat on child's head.

Take up folded double sheet that has sides cut off. Place it with fold at top. Fold inward a flap about 2¹/₂ inches on right side. Fold left half over right so as to make a square. Open figure out again.

Grasp at A with left fingers; this will be tip of cone-shaped hat. Grasp at B with right fingers and roll inward until it meets C. Let D come to E and G come to BC. Now tuck the flap in; there will also be a triangular corner that sticks out below; tuck that in as well. Make some stars on the hat with a marking pen.

Give the wizard hat to a child.

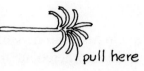

pull here

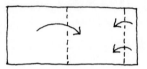

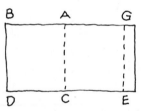

B   A   G

D   C   E

A   G

C B D E

tuck i

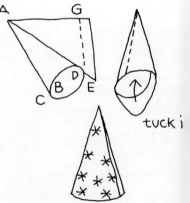

"Why don't you go off to the sea and sail away on a ship?" the younger sister suggested to her brother.

The young man thought that was good advice. He said good-bye to his younger sister and little brother and made his way to a seaport.

He saw boats and ships of many kinds, but at last he saw a ship that pleased him. It was a fine sailing ship. He signed up with the captain to go on a long voyage.

Take up single sheet that is square size. Find center point by folding horizontally, opening out, then vertically. Then fold all four corners to center point.

Turn figure over and again fold all four corners to center point. Turn figure over and once more fold all four corners to center point. Now open up figure and shape it as though it were a square table spread with a cloth.

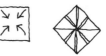
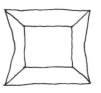

Flatten each of the corner points to the sides of the square in clockwise fashion, so that you end up with a pinwheel. Now fold the figure in half, diagonally.

Lift up the point sticking down below and fold it back, parallel to the boat's keel. You now have a sailboat.

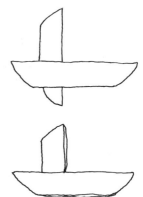

Hand it to one of the children.

They sailed away until they came to Mexico. The young man liked it there so much he said: "Someday I want to bring my sister and brother to see all these interesting things."

To remember the fine time he had in Mexico, he went out and bought many souvenirs and gifts.

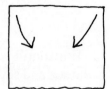

Take up one of folded-down single sheets. With fold at top, bring upper corners to middle so they meet exactly. Fold down. Fold up top layer of lower flap, halfway. Fold up again; tuck ends behind triangle.

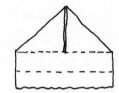

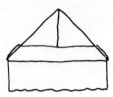

Turn figure over. Repeat two folds on lower flap. Open triangle; bring A to B and flatten out to make square figure.

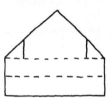

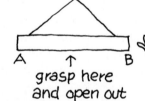

A   ↑   B
grasp here
and open out

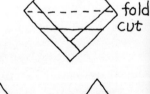

Cut off triangles with sides of about 2¹/₂ inches, from open points of square. Fold up remaining base of triangle. Turn figure over and fold up that base as well.

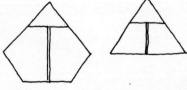

His favorite was a large, black sombrero. He did not know that it was a magic sombrero.

When he came back home after the long voyage, the owner of the ship said: "You are such a fine navigator that I am going to make you captain of your own ship."

He put a captain's hat on the young man's head. So the young man went back to Krakow, kissed his sister and gave the sombrero to his little brother. "Wish me luck!" he said, and off he went, back to the seaport. When he got there, it was not another sailing ship that awaited him, but a big steamship, with a funnel.

Gently pull sides apart. Press in crown as though shaping a man's felt hat. Pull rim away from crown. You will have a sombrero. Put it on head of the child who is captain.

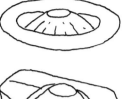

Take up second folded-down single sheet. Repeat all movements as for sombrero, above, up to the point of cutting off the triangles. Instead of cutting off these points, fold them up to top corner. Open out and you have the captain's hat.

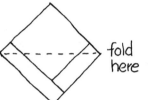

Give captain's hat to child representing captain and pass sombrero to child who represents younger brother or sister.

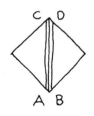

Take up last folded-over single sheet. Repeat all folds as for captain's hat. Now gently open up the hat until A reaches B. Do not press down the folds of the resulting new square; instead, grasp C and D and pull apart. You will get a steamship with a funnel.

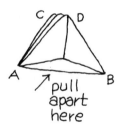

"I'm willing, if you're willing," said the young captain from Krakow. He guided his ship into the North Sea and was on his way. He was a good captain, but even the best of captains sometimes has bad luck.

One night as the ship was moving along, it bumped right into an iceberg. That tore out a big chunk from the bow. The bump sent the ship backward in a half-circle, and there was another iceberg! It smashed into the stern and tore a huge piece off.

This was too much for the ship's steam engine. The boiler burst and the funnel blew its top. The ship started to sink, so the captain ordered all his men into the lifeboats. He would wait until everyone was off and safe before he left the ship. But it was too late! The ship sank, and the captain found himself in the icy cold water. Now I'm done for, he thought.

Take firm hold of steamship figure and tear off the bow.

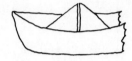

Turn ship around and tear off the other end piece, the stern.

Tear off the top of the funnel.

Back at home, his little brother and younger sister were playing. They were pretending they were on a visit to Mexico. The brother had on the sombrero. Now, you haven't forgotten that it was a magic sombrero, have you? Well, that magic sombrero began to tingle and itch so that the little brother knew something was wrong. "I think our brother is in danger," he said. The sister put on her wizard hat and worked a magic spell.

At that very moment, the captain, who was floundering in the sea, saw in front of him a life vest just his size. He put it on and soon his men saw him and picked him up. When the captain went back home to Krakow for a rest, his brother and sister told him how they had saved him. So he asked them to always wear the magic sombrero and the wizard hat, whenever he was at sea.

Open out torn-up steamship. You will have a life vest. Put it on child who is the captain.

101

A Finger Story to Tell When Traveling to Other Countries
by Ruth Stotter

This simple tale is very easy to learn and almost never fails to tickle the sense of humor of children from three to ten or so, of any nationality. If you cannot learn all of the words in the sentences or phrases given in the foreign languages below, then learn just the key words for "Baby," "Mama," "Papa," "Grandfather," "Grandmother," and "Don't touch!" This will be enough to get you by. Say the other words in English.

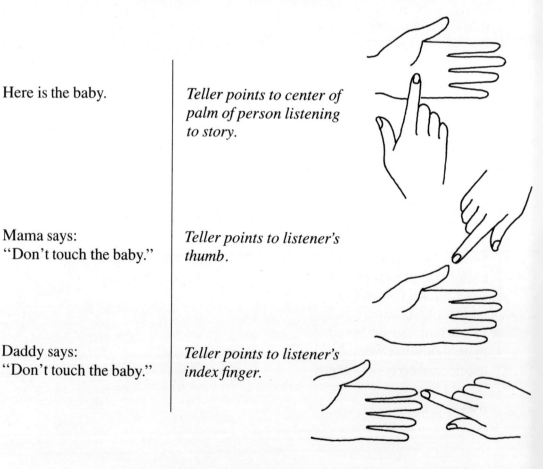

Here is the baby.	*Teller points to center of palm of person listening to story.*
Mama says: "Don't touch the baby."	*Teller points to listener's thumb.*
Daddy says: "Don't touch the baby."	*Teller points to listener's index finger.*

	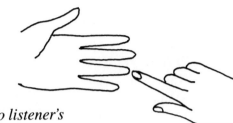
Grandfather says: "Don't touch the baby."	*Teller points to listener's* *middle finger.*
	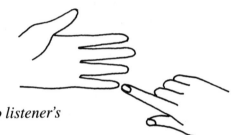
Grandmother says: "Don't touch the baby."	*Teller points to listener's* *ring finger.*
Sister says: "Don't touch the baby."	*Teller points to listener's* *little finger.*
Now, do you remember —where is the baby?	*Teller waits. Listener* *will usually reach out* *with other hand and* *touch palm with a finger.*
Don't touch the baby!	*Teller lightly slaps the* *hand with which listener* *has "touched the baby."* 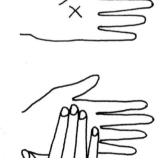

Here is the same story, in a number of other languages. Some are given only phonetically; since I cannot read the original language, friends and acquaintances simply helped me write them out as they would sound. The phrase "Don't touch the baby!" is given only once; repeat it each time you see (repeat).

SPANISH

Aquí está el bébé. — *Ah-kée ess-táh ell báy-báy.*
Mamá dice: — *Ma-má dée-say:*
No toquela el bébé! — *No tóh-kay-lah ell báy-báy!*
Papá dice: (repeat) — *Pa-pá dée-say:*
Abuelo dice: (repeat) — *Ah-bẃay-loh dée-say:*
Abuela dice: (repeat) — *Ah-bẃay-lah dée-say:*
Hermana dice: (repeat) — *Air-máh-nah dée-say:*
Bueno, donde está el bébé? — *Bẃay-noh, dóan-day ess-táh ell báy-báy?*

Puedes mostrarme? — *Pẃay-thess moh-stráhr-may?*
  (repeat)

FRENCH

Voilà le bébé. — *Vwah-láh luh báy-báy.*
Mama dit: — *Mah-máh dee:*
Ne touche pas le bébé! — *Nuh toosh pah luh báy-báy!*
Papa dit: (repeat) — *Pah-páh dee:*
Grand-père dit: (repeat) — *Grawhn-páir dee:*
Grand-mère dit: (repeat) — *Grawhn-mare dee:*
La soeur dit: (repeat) — *Lah sir dee:*
Alors, est-ce que tu te souviens où est le bébé? — *Ah-lóre, eh-suh kuh tue tuh sue-vyenne ou eh luh báy-báy?*
Tu peux me montrer? — *Tue puh muh moan-tráy?*
  (repeat)

GERMAN

Hier ist das Baby.
Mutter sagt:
Fass das Baby nicht an!
Vater sagt: (repeat)
Grossvater sagt: (repeat)
Grossmutter sagt: (repeat)
Schwester sagt: (repeat)
So, weisst du noch, wo das
    Baby ist?
Zeig mir mal!
    (repeat)

Here isst dahss báy-bee.
Múh-ter zahkt:
Fahss dahss báy-bee nicht
    ahn!
Fáh-ter zahkt:
Grohss-fah-ter zahkt:
Grohss-muh-ter zahkt:
Shvéss-ter zahkt:
So, vye-sst due nohkh, voh
    dahss báy-bee isst?
Tsyke meer mahl!

RUSSIAN

Voht ree-byóh-nok.
Mah-máh gah-vah-réet:
Nyeh troh-gúy ree-byóhn-kah!
Pah-páh gah-vah-réet: (repeat)
Dyéh-doosh-kah gah-vah-réet:
    (repeat)
Báh-boosh-kah gah-vah-réet:
    (repeat)
Shéh-strah gah-vah-réet: (repeat)
Tee-pyáir, tee pohm-neesh gdeh
    ree-byóh-nok?
Móh-zheesh tee poh-kah-zhát
    mnyeh?
    (repeat)

CZECH

Zdeh yeh mah-leh dee-teh.
Maht-kah zhee-káh:
Neh-doh-tee-kye dee-teh!
Tah-tah zhee-káh: (repeat)
Déh-deh-chek zhee-káh: (repeat)

Báh-beech-kah zhee-káh: (repeat)

Séss-strah zhee-káh: (repeat)
Pah, mah-too-yesh see kdeh yeh
    dee-teh?
    (repeat)

HUNGARIAN

Itt van a kisbaba!
Edes anya mondja:
Ne nyulj a kisbabahoz!
Edes apa mondja: (repeat)
Nagypapa mondja: (repeat)
Nagymama mondja: (repeat)
Nover mondja: (repeat)
Namost emlekszel hol van a
    kisbaba?
Meg tudod mutatni nekem?
    (repeat)

POLISH

Óh-toh yest dzheh-chée-nah.
Máht-kah múh-vyeh:
Nyeh doh-tee-kotch dzeh-chée-nah!
Óy-chetz múh-vyeh: (repeat)
Dzhýa-deck múh-vyeh: (repeat)
Bahb-kah múh-vyeh: (repeat)
Shýoh-strah múh-vyeh: (repeat)
Téh-rahz vyésh, gdzheh yest dzheh-
    chée-nah?
Mohzh-esh mnyeh poh-kah-zátz?
    (repeat)

JAPANESE

Koh-koh deh-su-kah
    ah-kah-chahn.
Oh-ka-a-sahn gah:
Ah-kah-chahn-oh sah-wah-rah-
    nah-ee-deh, koo-dah sah-ee!
Oh-toh-oh-sahn gah: (repeat)
Oh-jee-ee-chahn gah: (repeat)
Oh-bah-ah-chahn gah: (repeat)
Oh-nee-ee-sahn gah: (repeat)
Ah-kah-chahn, wah, ee-mah
    doh-koh deh-suh-kah?
    (repeat)

CHINESE

Wah-wah tzeye dtzur-ee.

Mama seul:
Boo-yao pun wah-wah!

Baba seul: (repeat)
Kong-kong seul: (repeat)
Neye-neye seul: (repeat)
May-may seul: (repeat)
Wah-wah tzeye nah-ree?
    (repeat)

Stories with Objects

If you have unusual objects that come from other countries or items that have been handed down in your family and therefore have special meaning, use them in short story sessions. This is a much better way to tell children how precious the objects are to you, and why you want them handled carefully. The following are only a few suggestions. Look around your home for other items.

THE FIVE CLEVER GIRLS:
A Nesting Doll Story

Materials needed: a set of five dolls that fit inside each other; four may also be used, in which case you must drop one of the riddles. I got the idea for this story from an old collection of medieval tales researched by Albert Wesselski; I added to it by taking riddles that have been passed down for generations in Europe. Most of the riddles I found in the study done by Jan de Vries, *Die Märchen von Klugen Rätsellösern.*

There was once a man named Gonella who made his living by tricking people. He would go from town to town and every day he ended up with his belly full of food and his pockets full of coins, all earned by his tricks. One day, Gonella set off down a road he'd never traveled before. In the distance he saw a town. When he came to the edge of town, there was a house, and in front of it stood a young girl.

Show doll set closed up.

107

She didn't look any too bright, so Gonella thought to himself: I'm sure I can find someone to trick here. Aloud, he said to the girl: "Good day, miss, where is your father?" "Good day, sir," she replied politely. "My father is busy. He is busy making many out of few."

Gonella didn't understand her answer, but he didn't say so out loud. Hmm, he thought to himself, perhaps there is someone else here who will give me a straight answer. Just at that moment, from behind the girl stepped—her younger sister. Gonella stepped up to her and spoke: "Good day, miss! Where is your mother?"

The second girl answered just as politely: "Good day, sir! My mother is busy. She is busy making something better out of something good." Gonella was puzzled. He did not understand that answer, either; but he was not about to admit it.

Just then, from behind that girl stepped another younger sister. "Good day to you, young lady! Where is your brother?"

The third girl was as polite as her sisters: "Good morning, sir! My brother is busy. He is busy hunting between heaven and earth."

Quickly take apart biggest doll, put top and bottom together, and set aside on table or other visible place. Show second doll.

Take off second largest doll, put top and bottom together, and set next to biggest doll. Show third doll.

Are these girls trying to fool me? wondered Gonella. He decided he'd better go to another house to find someone to trick. But just then, from behind the third sister stepped a still younger one. She was quite small. She will surely give something away, thought Gonella. He spoke to her: "Good day, little girl! Where is your grandfather?"

The fourth sister replied politely: "Good day, sir. My grandfather is busy. He is busy closing the door to keep it open."

These girls are all answering me with riddles, said Gonella to himself. He was ready to turn and move on to another house in the town. But just then, from behind the fourth girl stepped—the baby of the family. She was so small, she could hardly walk and talk. Maybe she will point out to me where someone is, said Gonella to himself. I might as well ask her. He simpered up to the little girl: "Hello there, my sweet little one! Where is your granny?"

"Granny is busy," said the littlest girl. "She is busy baking bread we already ate."

That was too much for Gonella. He exploded: "You girls are naughty. You are all telling me lies!"

Take apart third doll, put top and bottom together, and set next to first two dolls. Show fourth doll.

Take apart fourth doll, put top and bottom together, and set next to first three dolls. Show fifth doll at precisely the moment you mention "the baby of the family."

"Oh, no, sir!" cried the littlest one. "We are telling you the truth. Can't you smell?"

Gonella sniffed. He could smell the delicious smell of bread baking. "But how could it be bread you've already eaten?" he asked.

The little girl explained: "Yesterday, Granny saw we had no more bread in the house, so she sent us to the neighbor to borrow five loaves. But we were so hungry, we ate them all up. This morning, Granny started making bread. She made five round loaves. She had the bread in the oven when she remembered something. 'Oh, my,' she said, 'I only made five loaves and now I remember that we must give back that many to our neighbor. I'm baking bread we already ate. As soon as it's done I must make some more.' So you see, I was telling the truth: Granny is baking bread we already ate."

What a clever answer for such a little girl, thought Gonella to himself. But he did not say so aloud. Instead, he thought to himself: I'd better find out what those other girls meant by their answers. Then no one can fool me with them in the future.

Put down smallest doll.

He went to the next oldest girl and asked: "What was that again about your grandfather?"

"He's busy closing the door to keep it open."

"How could he be doing that?"

The little girl pointed to a spot by the river. "There is Grandfather. He is mending the fish net where we keep the fish we hope to eat. Yesterday, one of the fish made a big hole in the net, and Grandfather said it was like a door, letting out the other fish. He said he must close that door, so the fish wouldn't get away. But he dare not close it up too tight, because then the fish couldn't swim and breathe. They would die and we can't eat dead fish. So Grandfather said he had to close the door in the fish net, just enough to keep it open."

Well, I've never heard the like, thought Gonella. He went to the next girl. "What was that about your brother?"

"He's hunting between heaven and earth." Gonella looked around. He saw no sign of the brother.

"There he is," cried the girl, pointing up to one of the trees. "He's up in the

Pick up fourth doll.

Put down fourth doll and pick up third doll.

111

cherry tree, hunting for the sweetest cherries. He's not up in heaven, and he's not on earth. He's hunting between heaven and earth."

Gonella went to the next girl. "What was that again about your mother?"

"She is making something better out of something good."

Gonella looked up. He looked down. He did hear a thumping sound, but he saw no sign of the mother.

The girl pointed to a building at the side of the house. "Mother is in the dairy, churning cream into butter. Cream is good, but butter is better."

"I would have figured that out, if only you had let me listen a bit longer," said Gonella. He went to the last girl. "What was it you said about your father?"

"He's busy making many out of few," she answered.

Gonella looked up, down, and all around. He smelled and he listened. But he still could not figure it out.

"Father is way out there, in our field. He is planting seeds. For every seed he plants, we will harvest a hundred grains. He is making many out of few."

Put down third doll and pick up second doll.

Put down second doll and pick up first doll.

Well, thought Gonella to himself, if the children in this place are so clever, what must the grown-ups be like? I don't think I can find anyone to trick here. He turned and walked off in the opposite direction and never came back. And that is how five clever girls saved their town from being tricked by Gonella.

Put down first doll and point to all five of them.

Allow the children to put the doll set back together again.

(See Part Three for suggestions on using nesting dolls to tell family stories.)

GRANDMOTHER'S APRONS: A Quilt Story

Materials needed: 9 squares of cloth: 1 each of white, red, yellow, blue, green, pink, and brown; as well as 1 of red-white-and-blue (striped pattern is best) and one of yellow balls or circles on a blue background. I like to use squares of about 8 inches each, but smaller and larger sizes work well, too. Once, when I was telling at the Hillcrest School in Toronto, the children requested a quilt story. I didn't happen to have my cloth squares, but I did have a lot of origami paper, and I substituted that. It worked fairly well, but my first choice would always be cloth.

This story was inspired by Blanche Losinski, a friend and contemporary of my parents, who was for many years a teacher and then a superintendent of schools in Wisconsin. She shared with me many of her family stories, and among them was a wonderful reminiscence about her grandmother's and mother's aprons. I have taken some of her memories, added my own to them, and created this story. If you have an heirloom quilt in your family, and would like to substitute other stories, but use the basic idea given here, feel free to do so.

Have pile of cloth squares ready, in this order: white, yellow circles on blue, yellow, pink, green, red-white-blue, brown, red, blue.

About seventy years ago, John was a little boy growing up in the city. But his grandmother and grandfather lived on a farm and every summer John went to live with them for a few weeks.

Every day, before starting their work, Grandfather would put on his overalls and Grandmother put on an apron. Some of Grandmother's aprons were plain white; others were made of colorful cloth.

One rainy day, John was angry that he couldn't play outside.

'Where is the sun?" he asked crossly. "I want it to shine so I can go out."

Grandmother smiled and said: "I will make a secret little playhouse for you, where there will be many suns shining." She placed two chairs so that their backs were a few feet apart. Then she took off her apron. It was blue with yellow suns all over it.

Hold up square of blue with yellow balls or circles.

Grandmother spread the apron over the backs of the two chairs. It made a cozy little house. John went inside and played happily for the rest of the day.

The next day the sun shone again. Grandmother wore a clean white apron. Late that morning she said it was time to collect the eggs. She asked John to help her.

They went to the henhouse. The chickens were cackling and clucking. Grandmother gathered her apron into one hand, so that it made a basket. With the other hand she reached into the nests, picked up the eggs, and put them in her apron basket. Sometimes she had to reach right under one of the hens.

"I want to do that once," said John. He put his hand under a fat, white hen so he could get the eggs. The hen snapped at him with her sharp beak. It scared John so much, he threw the egg into Grandmother's apron, on top of the other eggs. They broke and splashed deep yellow yolk all over the white apron. Later, when Grandmother tried to wash it out, the apron still had yellow yolk spots.

"Never mind," she said. "I always wanted a yellow apron." And she dyed it bright yellow, so the stains hardly showed.

Hold up yellow square. Then put it aside.

One day Grandmother, Grandfather, and John went for a walk in the woods. They came upon a patch of ripe wild strawberries. "I wish I'd brought my berry basket," said Grandmother. "Then we could pick some of these berries."

"You *have* a basket," said John. He pointed to Grandmother's white apron. So they picked berries and carried them home in the apron basket. When they emptied the apron, they saw that the juice had run out of some of the berries. Parts of the apron were now strawberry pink.

"Well, I've always wanted a pink apron," said Grandmother, and she dyed it pink.

Hold up pink square. Then put it down.

One Sunday they went on a picnic, but they forgot the old blanket to sit on. There were ants and bugs crawling in the grass. John didn't want to sit down and eat. "We'll sit on this blanket," said Grandmother, and she spread out her Sunday apron, a white one trimmed with lace. When they had finished eating, and picked up the apron, they saw it was covered with green grass stains.

"Hmmm," said Grandmother. "A green apron might be just as pretty." So she dyed it green.

Hold up green square. Then set it aside.

On the Fourth of July they went to town to see Grandfather march in the parade. He wore his old army uniform. Many of the other people had small flags to wave. John did not have one.

"I wish I had a flag to wave at Grandfather," he said.

"Here's a flag for you," said Grandmother. She took off the red-white-and-blue apron that she was wearing to feel patriotic.

Hold up red-white-and-blue square. Wave it like a flag.

It was big enough for John and Grandmother to wave at Grandfather as he passed by. In fact, it was the biggest flag there.

Every Saturday, Grandfather shined his shoes. He sat down on a bench in the front yard, spread the polish on each shoe, and then buffed the shoes with a soft cloth. One Saturday, Grandfather asked John to run and ask Grandmother for a shoe-polishing rag. John looked in the kitchen, but Grandmother was not there. He knew she always took cleaning rags from a drawer in the kitchen. So, he opened the drawer and took out a big white cloth. He ran out and took it to Grandfather.

Without unfolding it, Grandfather buffed and polished his shoes until they were a shiny, smooth brown. Then he did the same with John's shoes. Just then, Grandmother came up. "What are you doing with my apron?" she cried. The apron was covered with brown streaks of shoe polish.

"I found it in your rag drawer," said John.

At first Grandmother looked annoyed. Then she shook her head and laughed. "One can always use a nice, brown apron," she said, and she dyed it brown.

Hold up brown square. Then set it down.

John liked going barefoot. In town he had to wear shoes, but on the farm he could go barefoot all he liked. But sometimes he did not watch out where he was walking. One day he stepped on a piece of sharp glass. It made a deep gash in his foot. He ran to his grandmother, crying. Quickly, she took off her white apron and wound it around John's foot. Then she carried him to the house.

"It's not too bad," said Grandmother after she had washed out the cut. "You bled a lot, but that's good because it washes out the dirt that might have gotten in." She sat John in the rocking chair in the kitchen for the rest of the afternoon and told him stories while she cooked supper.

Her apron had big splotches of red right in the middle. "I suppose I could soak it and boil it out," said Grandmother, "but I'd kind of like to have a red apron, anyway." And she dyed this apron red.

Hold up red square. Then set aside.

All too soon, the time came for John to go back home. He couldn't wait to tell his parents about all the things that had happened on the farm. It was a long ride into town. They went by horse and buggy. It grew dark and John felt chilly. He shivered.

Grandmother took off her beautiful going-to-town apron of deep, soft blue.

Hold up blue square. Then set aside.

She put it around John. By the time they got to his house in town, he was fast asleep.

Now when John grew up, he married and had children of his own. His grandmother and grandfather became old and died, but John never forgot them. After many years, John himself became a grandfather. Sometimes

116

he liked to prepare a meal of barbecued hamburgers or chicken. Before he started, he always put on one of his grandmother's old white aprons.

But best of all, he liked to tell stories to his grandchildren. He would tuck them into bed under a quilt, and then he would point to the colorful patches in the quilt, one by one, and tell them what had happened a long time ago, when the squares had been pieces of his grandmother's aprons.

He told them about the time she made him a sunshiny playhouse on a rainy day.

Start laying out squares in quilt-like pattern. I usually like to place them in three rows of three, with the sun-in-blue-sky square in the middle. I then encourage the child listeners to tell me the story that each square represents, by simply starting out with the phrase,

He told them about . . .

Place the squares, one by one, in any order you like. Usually, I end with the deep blue square. I can then close the story with one of these endings:

And I'm sleepy, too, so it's time to say good-night and turn out the light.

or

Now, since everyone in the story is sleeping, it's time for us to leave them quietly and put our squares away.

THE WATER CUP

as told by Ruth Stotter

Materials needed: A cup or mug, full of water. It can be especially appropriate if the cup is a family heirloom. I learned this as a teen-ager, by word of mouth. I cannot remember who it was that first told me the story. I only know that it went the rounds, with each one of us vying to be the first to see if we could get a particular person to fall for it and attempt to drink water from the far side of the cup. I have changed it here, because I noticed that children find it supremely funny if the storyteller lets herself get splashed by the water from the cup. You may, of course, substitute "old woman," or "my father" or "my mother" for "the old man." If you wish to make believe it happened to you, make all the appropriate substitutions, even inventing other things that were willed to your real siblings.

When the old man lay dying he called for his three sons. To the oldest he gave his money. To the second, his land and possessions. Then, turning to the third son, he said: "My son, I have no more property to leave you, no gold or jewels. All I have, my son, is this cup.

Hold cup up for everyone to see.

"This cup belonged to your great-great-grandfather, who gave it to your great-grandfather, who gave it to your grandfather, who gave it to me. And now I give it to you. I would hope that you will pass this cup on to your children. But, my son, you must remember *never* to drink out of this side of this special cup.

Point to side farthest from you.

"Always drink from this side."

Point to side closest to you.

"Why is that, Father?"

"Son, just listen and pay attention to your elders. It is mandatory, imperative that you always drink out of *this* side of the cup."

Point again to closest side.

"But, Father, I don't understand."

"Son, there is nothing to understand. Just never, ever, under any circumstances whatsoever, drink out of this side of the cup."

Point again to far side.

"Father, it doesn't make any sense."

"Please, my son, I am dying. I am an old man. Just respect my words of wisdom. I will tell you one more time. When you drink out of this cup *always* drink out of *this* side—

Point to closest side.

and never out of *this* side."

Point to far side.

"But Father, what would happen if I *were* to drink out of that side?"

"My son, if you were to drink out of that side—

Point to far side.

then—

Slowly pick up cup and drink from the rim on the outside.

water will spill all over you!"

Drawing Stories in Sand, Snow, or Mud

As mentioned in the last section of Part Three, girls and young women of many Eskimo groups in Southwestern Alaska like very much to draw pictures as they tell stories to each other. In fact, Lynn Price Ager, who has studied storyknifing among these groups, mentions that girls become so used to drawing while storytelling that, when they are adults, they often move their hands in drawing patterns as they tell or speak.

The story almost always begins by setting the place. A home is drawn, and the basic furnishings are sketched in. Then the characters are drawn in. There are a number of designs used for the different types of characters, but common ones found among the Napaskiak are:

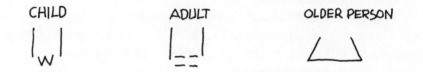

CHILD   ADULT   OLDER PERSON

Each time, before a character speaks, a V-like design is drawn in as a face:

Then, eyes, nose, and mouth are added:

When a character speaks again in the story, a stroke or two quotation marks are often added above the figure representing that character:

Sometimes the character is erased by smoothing over the snow, mud, or wet sand, either to indicate the character has moved on to other action, or to make room for the teller to draw something else. If the house scene gets too crowded, the teller sketches another house of the same type and continues the action there. Each piece of action is sketched out, too, unless it is too complex, in which case a few dots or strokes suggest something is going on. Not all Eskimo groups use the same designs or methods, but the girls in a given area generally tend to use the same methods and pictures so that they understand each other.

After explaining this custom, and demonstrating with a story such as the one that follows, you might like to make up stories set in your own cultural milieu. Change the drawings to match your surroundings. Or play the storyknifing game the way some Eskimo girls play it: In snow, sand, or mud, sketch out a home and its basic furnishings; then ask your audience to guess whose home it is. Keep adding clues to the sketches until they guess correctly.

THE GIRL WHO HAD SORES ON HER BODY

Materials needed: a stick or table knife; fresh snow, or a mud bank, or a wet, sandy beach, on which to draw. This is based on motifs found in the stories Wendell H. and Helen T. Oswalt collected among the Napaskiak Eskimo girls of Southwestern Alaska.

Once, long ago, there was an old style house.[1] It had an entry room attached at one side.[2] There was a tunnel that went from the entry room into the[3] house.

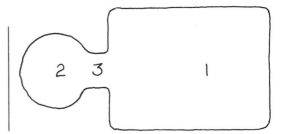

121

In the center of the entry[4] was a firepit, and there was a second firepit[5] in the main house. Along the walls inside the house were beds[6,7] and lounging areas.[8,9]

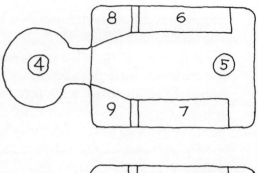

In the house there lived a grand-mother[10] and her three granddaugh-ters.[11,12,13]

ERASE 12←13

The two oldest girls often went out-side of the house. One day they said[14,15]: "Let's go sliding down the hill."

Another day they said: "Let's play at storyknifing."[16,17]

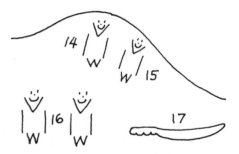

"Why don't you go outside?"[18] Grandmother asked the youngest girl.

"Because I am covered with sores," she said.[19] "The boys laugh at me and make me cry when I go out and play."

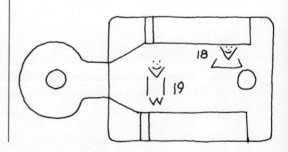

Grandmother called the oldest girl[20]: "Go and get some water from the river."

"All right,"[21] said the oldest girl. She went off with a large bowl to get water.[22] But before she got to the river, she saw a big thing behind the trees.[23] She was very scared so she ran home, without the water. "A big thing scared me," she said to Grandmother.[24] "I think it was a bear."

Grandmother said to the second girl: "You go and get water from the river."

"Yes, I'll go," said the second girl.[25]

She ran off with the bowl.[26] Before she got to the river, she saw a wolf. It was running back and forth.[27] That made the girl frightened so she ran back home.

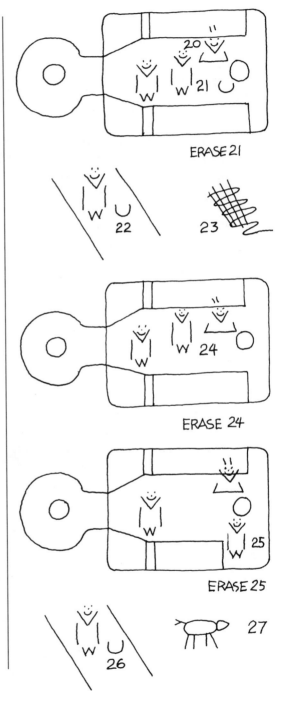

ERASE 21

ERASE 24

ERASE 25

123

"I didn't bring the water because a wolf scared me,"[28] said the second girl to her grandmother.

"Then you must go and get it yourself," Grandmother told the youngest girl.[29] The girl took her parka and stuffed it with grass. She put it outside on the far side of the house.[30] She made it look like a real girl.[31]

While the boys threw mud at it, she ran off to the river, carrying the bowl.[32] When she came to the river she stepped on stones[33] until she came to the clear, running water in the middle of the stream. She filled her bowl and started back.[34]

But the steppingstones were no longer there. She had no way to get back to shore. Down the river she saw a beaver. She sang[35] to the beaver and it brought wood[36] from its dam. The beaver laid the wood across the deep river[37] and the girl could cross over again.

She continued on her way home. Next she met an old man.[38] "Come to my house and cook my fish for me," he said.[39]

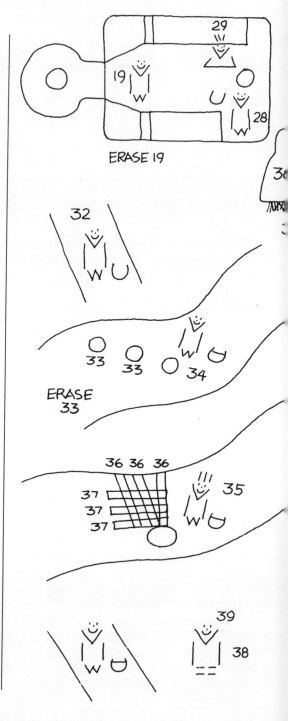

ERASE 19

ERASE 33

124

The girl went with him to his house.[40] She cooked fish for him to eat.[41] "Now go to sleep," said the man.[42] The girl lay down on one of the beds[43] but she did not sleep. She heard the man sharpening his knife.[44] "He is going to kill me as soon as I am asleep," she said.[45] "He will kill me and then eat me."

When his back was turned, she picked up her bowl of water[46] and slipped out of his house. She ran all the way back to her home,[47] where Grandmother was waiting.

"I must heat the water with herbs," said Grandmother.[48] When the water was hot, she bathed the sores of the youngest girl and gave her a fresh, clean dress to put on.[49] Then she gave her a new parka.[50]

"Now go to sleep," said Grandmother.[51] The girl went to bed.[52] She slept for a long time. When she woke up her sores were gone.

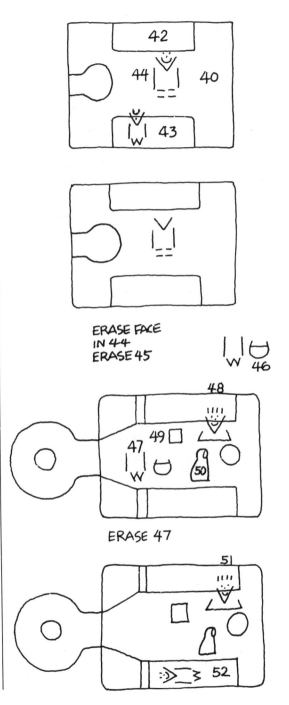

ERASE FACE IN 44
ERASE 45

ERASE 47

125

The Hungry Stranger:
A Buddhist Story from India
as retold by Ruth Stotter

This story shows that our environment and the culture we have often influence what we see. Most of us in Europe and North America have been trained to see "the Man in the Moon." However, in many parts of the world people see something different when they look up at the moon. For example, in some countries people see an owl, a woodcutter, or a girl carrying water buckets. The Native Americans of the Pacific Northwest see a frog or frog sisters on the moon. A rabbit or hare on the moon is in the tradition of much of India, Southeast Asia, and even parts of southern Africa. I learned this story by combining versions from several printed collections of Indian folk tales. Ever since I've been telling it, I can no longer see anything *but* the rabbit on the moon.

Materials needed: one sheet of plain white paper; juice of one lemon; toothpick; pen or colored pencil, candle, matches. Before beginning the story, draw a circle on the paper with the pen or colored pencil. Dip the toothpick in lemon juice and use it to make an outline profile of a rabbit

inside the circle. When the lemon juice dries, your drawing will be invisible. You are now ready to tell the story. Have the paper, the candle, and the matches handy.

Long ago, when the world was not as it is today, the great Buddha was born as a rabbit who lived in the forest. Every night he would meet his friends—Elephant, Otter, and Monkey.

One evening Rabbit said: "It may happen someday that a hungry person will come to our forest. If that happens, we should have something to offer him to eat. I have an idea. Tomorrow night let us each bring something that we could offer to a hungry passerby."

It was agreed. The next night Elephant brought figs, Monkey brought fresh mangoes, and Otter carried a fish. "What do you have, Rabbit?" they asked.

Rabbit showed them a pile of dry grass. The other animals thought this was funny, but they didn't want to hurt Rabbit's feelings, so they said nothing. But Rabbit knew what they were thinking, so he said: "I would never let anyone be hungry. I would always offer food to a hungry traveler."

Now it happened that the sky god Shakra heard this. "I will test Rabbit," he said to himself.

The next night Shakra disguised himself as an old beggar and visited the forest. When Elephant saw him, he offered his figs. Shakra shook his head: "I do not like fruit," he said.

He walked along until he came to the tree where Monkey was swinging. Monkey immediately offered his mangoes to the beggar. Again Shakra refused, and continued on his way.

He met Otter and Otter offered a fish. But Shakra shook his head, saying: "I am a vegetarian." Then he walked a bit further until he met up with Rabbit. "I am very hungry," he said.

Rabbit quickly pushed a pile of dry grass toward Shakra.

What! thought Shakra. Does Rabbit expect me to eat dried grass, like a cow?

Just then Rabbit lit the grass, and flames appeared (*light candle*).

What! thought Shakra. Does he expect me to eat burnt grass?

Then Rabbit got ready to jump into the fire. Now Shakra understood what a great gift Rabbit was prepared to offer.

"No, Rabbit," he said. "I am the god Shakra and I was testing you all, to see if you were sincere in promising food for any hungry creature. Now I want to do something for you."

Shakra took his own shape. He picked up a mountain in his mighty hands and squeezed it until a liquid came from its peak. Then Shakra reached up with the mountain peak, and, as though he were using a pen, he began to draw on the great round circle of the moon.

Show your paper with the circle. Then, carefully hold the circle over the candle, high enough so it doesn't catch fire but low enough in the smoke so that the lemon juice is heated and turns brown. Your rabbit drawing will magically appear.

When Rabbit looked up, he saw on the moon his picture—the outline of a rabbit. And you can see it there to this very day, or so the people of South Asia say. The next time there is a full moon, try to find the outline of the rabbit on the round face. And then you can tell someone else this story.

NOTE: You can tell this story around a campfire, holding the paper on a toasting stick, over the smoke. Lemon juice mystery notes can also be used to have the fire spirit reveal the title of this story, or other stories you wish to tell around the fire.

Bibliography

Included here are all items mentioned in the text, as well as material consulted for background information. Those items with an asterisk have indexes to stories, often by title, subject, and country of origin, and may be helpful in searching for particular types of stories.

A-dachi: A Japanese Paper-Folding Classic. Edited by J. L. Brossman and M. W. Brossman. Washington, D.C., Pinecone Press, 1961.

Ager, Lynn Price. "Storyknifing: An Alaskan Eskimo Girls' Game." *Journal of the Folklore Institute*, The Hague, Vol. 11, No. 3, 1975, pp. 187–98.

Anonymous. *Konstig en vermaakelijk tyd-verdryf der Hollandsche jufferen, of onderricht der papiere sny-kunst*. Amsterdam, Johannes ten Hoorn, 1686.

Bettelheim, Bruno. *The Uses of Enchantment: The Meaning and Importance of Fairy Tales*. New York, Alfred A. Knopf, 1976.

Blasche, B. H. *Der Papierformer, oder Anleitung, allerlei Gegenstände der Kunstwelt aus Papier nachzubilden*. Schnepfenthal, Buchhandlung der Erziehungsanstalt, 1819.

Blyth, Will. *Paper Magic*. London, Arthur Pearson, 191?

Braun-Ronsdorf, Margarete. *The History of the Handkerchief*. Leigh-on-Sea, England, F. Lewis, 1961.

Cammann, Alfred. *Westpreussischemärchen*. Berlin, W. de Gruyter, 1961.

Chase, Richard. *Grandfather Tales*. Boston, Houghton Mifflin, 1948.

Davis, Don, and Kay Stone. " 'To Ease The Heart:' Traditional Storytelling," *The National Storytelling Journal*, Vol. 1, No. 1, Winter 1984, pp. 3–6.

Favat, F. Andre. *Child and Tale: The Origins of Interest*. Urbana, Ill., National Council of Teachers of English, 1977.

Feynman, Richard P. "The Pleasure of Finding Things Out," "Nova" transcript, Program No. 1002. Boston, WGBH, 1983.

Ford, Z. *Paper Folding and Designing Combined*. Leeds, England, A. L. Educational Series, 1899.

Gardner, Richard A. *Therapeutic Communication with Children: The Mutual Storytelling Technique*. New York, Science House, 1971.

Goodman, James S. "Souvenirs," *The National Storytelling Journal*, Vol. 2, No. 4, Fall 1985.

Grumet, Robert S. *New World Encounters: Jasper Danckaerts' View of Indian Life in 17th-Century Brooklyn*. Brooklyn, N.Y., Brooklyn Historical Society, 1986.

"Die Hand im Kinderspiel." *Die Kärntner Landsmannschaft*, Heft 3, 1966, pp. 6–8.

Ho, Mobi. "A Vast Reservoir of Memories," *The National Storytelling Journal*, Vol. 1, No. 4, Fall 1984. Reprinted from *The National Catholic Reporter*.

Jacobs, Joseph. *English Folk and Fairy Tales*. New York, G. P. Putnam's Sons, n.d.

Jones, Bessie, and Bess Lomax Hawes. *For the Ancestors*. Urbana, Ill., University of Illinois Press, 1983.

*Kimmel, Margaret, and Elizabeth Segal. *For Reading Out Loud: A Guide to Sharing Books with Children*. New York, Delacorte, 1983.

Latter, Lucy R. *How to Teach Paper-Folding*. New York, E. L. Kellogg, 1899.

Leske, Marie. *Illustriertes Spielbuch für Mädchen*. Leipzig, Otto Spamer, 1871.

Livo, Norma. "The Golden Spoon: Preserving Family History," *The National Storytelling Journal*, Vol. 1, No. 3, Summer 1984, pp. 8–10.

*MacDonald, Margaret Read. *The Storyteller's Sourcebook: A Subject, Title, and Motif Index to Folklore Collections for Children*. Detroit, Gale, 1982.

The National Storytelling Journal, Jonesborough, Tenn., National Association for the Preservation and Perpetuation of Storytelling, 1984–present.

Olson, Glending. *Literature as Recreation in the Later Middle Ages*. Ithaca, N.Y., Cornell University Press, 1982.

Oswalt, Wendell H., and Helen T. Oswalt. "Traditional Storyknife Tales of Yuk Girls," *Proceedings of the American Philosophical Society*, Vol. 108, No. 4, Aug. 1964, pp. 310–336.

Paper Innovations: Handmade Paper and Handmade Objects of Cut, Folded, and Molded Paper. Edited by Martha Longenecker. La Jolla, Calif., Mingei International Museum of World Folk Art, 1985.

Pellowski, Anne. *The World of Storytelling*. New York, R. R. Bowker, 1977.

———. *Stairstep Farm: Anna Rose's Story*. New York, Philomel, 1981.

———. *The Story Vine: A Source Book of Unusual and Easy-to-Tell Stories from Around the World*. New York, Macmillan, 1984.

Peters-Holger, Katherina. *Das Taschentuch; eine theatergeschichtliche Studie*. Emsdetten, Westfalen, Verlag Lechte, 1961.

Ransome, Arthur. *Old Peter's Russian Tales*. London, Nelson, 1916.

Sayers, Frances Clarke. "From Me to You." In *Summoned by Books*. New York, The Viking Press, 1965.

Segun, Mabel. *My Father's Daughter*. Lagos, African Universities Press, 1965 (African Readers Series).

Singer, Isaac Bashevis. *Naftali the Storyteller and His Horse, Sus*. New York, Farrar, Straus & Giroux, 1976.

————. *The Power of Light: Eight Stories for Hanukkah*. New York, Farrar, Straus & Giroux, 1980.

Skinner, B. F., and M. E. Vaughan. *Enjoy Old Age: A Program of Self-Management*. New York, W. W. Norton, 1983.

Sperl, J. *Handbuchlein der Papierfaltekunst*. Leipzig, Hartleben, 1904.

Stone, Kay. "Lying in Public," *The National Storytelling Journal*. Vol. 1, No. 3, Summer 1984, pp. 22–23.

Stories: A List of Stories to Tell and to Read Aloud. 7th ed. Edited by Marilyn Berg Iarusso, New York, The New York Public Library, 1977.

Stories to Tell: A List of Stories with Annotations. 5th ed. Edited by Jeanne Hardendorff. Baltimore, Enoch Pratt Free Library, 1965.

Stories to Tell Children: A Selected List. 8th ed. Edited by Laura Cathon. Pittsburgh, University of Pittsburgh Press, 1974.

Taschentuch in Tracht und Brauch; Volkskunde, Fakten und Analysen. Wien, Verein für Volkskunde, 1972.

Théo, R. *De schaduwbeelden of figuren welke bijmiddel met de hand kunnen uitgevoerd worden*. Gent, Snoeck-Ducaju, 189?.

*Trelease, Jim. *The Read-Aloud Handbook*. 2nd ed. New York, Viking Penguin, Inc., 1985.

Van Breda, A. *Plezier met papier*. Amsterdam, Uitgeverij Van Breda, n.d.

Vries, Jan de. *Die Märchen des klugen Rätsellösern*. Helsinki, Folklore Fellows Communications, No. 73, 1928.

Wade, Barrie. *Story at Home and School*. University of Birmingham, Educational Review Occasional Publications, No. 10, n.d.

Wesselski, Albert. *Die Begebenheiten der beiden Gonnella*. Weimar, 1920.

Wolfenstein, Martha. *Children's Humor*. Glencoe, Ill., The Free Press, 1954.

Wrightson, Patricia. "The Geranium Leaf," *Horn Book Magazine*, Vol. 62, No. 2, Mar.–Apr. 1986, pp. 176–85.

Yolen, Jane. *Touch Magic*. New York, Philomel, 1981.

Additional Sources of Good Stories to Tell

There are numerous story selection lists and books that are used by librarians and teachers to find stories that suit a particular thematic need. These aids are marked with an asterisk in the bibliography. The stories listed here are generally not found in the usual selection aids. I have tried to single out stories that suit an intimate family setting rather than those that work well with large public groups. However, a number of the stories cited here work equally well in both situations.

My intention was to include stories that would suit all age groups, but with emphasis on those for younger children. I would like to hear from those who have tried out these and other stories, in a family setting. I am especially interested to find out under what circumstances the stories were told, and what the audience reaction was.

Some of these books are readily available, but others have been out of print for some time. However, in many cases they can be found in your local public library, or located through inter-library loan.

On the whole, the children's books I looked at in mass market stores and chain bookstores do not have good stories for telling. Most of these are for reading aloud to the child, and depend heavily on color and picture for their appeal. The Mother Goose rhyme books were satisfactory, but the fairy-tale collections too often used mediocre language, or edited the original stories so much they were barely recognizable. Also, many of the fairy-tale collections are put together with no regard for the types of stories liked by children in the various stages they go through from about age two to age nine. The parent or adult must be very selective in choosing stories to tell from these collections.

I also looked at the selections available in several of the bookstores specializing only in children's books. The quality and range was much better, especially in the area of folk and fairy tales, rhymes, and special collections for storytellers. Therefore, if you wish to purchase books for use in storytelling with your children, I recommend you use one of these specialty stores. A complete listing of them, with addresses, can be obtained by sending a stamped, self-addressed envelope to the Association of Booksellers for Children, 826 S. Aiken Avenue, Pittsburgh, PA 15232.

General Collections of Stories for the Very Young

A Celebration of American Family Folklore: Tales and Traditions from the Smithsonian Collection. Edited by Steven J. Zeitlin, Amy J. Kotkin, and Holly Cutting Baker. New York, Pantheon Books, 1982.

This is an outstanding source book and would be the first I would recommend to any family genuinely interested in exploring their family stories. The short anecdotes shared by ordinary persons, showing how storytelling has been important in their lives, can give numerous ideas as to how and when stories can be introduced into daily life. The section on "Stories for Children," pages 126–145, would be especially helpful. It is also a joy to read, because of its and genuinely expressed sentiments. The material comes mostly from the interviews of persons who have attended the Festival of American Folklife in the past.

Colwell, Eileen. *Tell Me a Story*. London, Penguin Books, 1962.
————. *Tell Me Another Story*. London, Penguin Books, 1964.

The storyteller-collector indicates these are for children under five (the first volume) and children four to six (the second volume). The stories are mostly British in origin and are for those who wish to emphasize very traditional values. Some folk tales are included, as well as a generous selection of story poems.

Mitchell, Lucy Sprague. *Believe and Make-Believe*. New York, E. P. Dutton, 1956.

This collection of stories is selected from early issues of *Humpty Dumpty's Magazine* and from the experiences of writers and teachers working with children at the Bank Street College of Education. The emphasis is on stories that make it easy for children to distinguish the world of fantasy from the world of reality. There are, however, a few stories that combine both.

I like especially "The Bread Cloud" by Lois Salk Galpern, which could be used before or after a visit to a bakery. "A Sack of Potatoes" by Rita S. Cooper is the type of story easily learned by any adult playing with a young child who is just beyond the stage of peek-a-boo but not quite ready for hide-and-seek. "Guess What's in the Grass" by Lucy Sprague Mitchell is another effective guess-where-I'm-hiding type story. It could be told while out on a summer walk.

The story "Cheese, Peas, and Chocolate Pudding," by Betty Van Witsen, mentioned in Part Two, can be found in this Mitchell book. It is also in the collection *It's Time for Story Hour*, compiled by Elizabeth H. Sechrist and Jeanette Woolsey, Philadelphia, Macrae Smith, 1964.

Mitchell, Lucy Sprague. *Here and Now Storybook*. New York, E. P. Dutton, 1921.

Mrs. Mitchell believed that young children need stories of the present just as much as (or perhaps more than) they need stories of a fantasy or fairy-tale-like world. She assembled this collection after testing out many stories with young children at the Bank Street College of Education. Those adults who are not particularly attracted to fairy tales might like to read Mrs. Mitchell's philosophy with regard to stories, as summarized in her introduction.

Shedd, Charlie, and Martha Shedd. *Tell Me a Story; Stories for Your Grandchildren and the Art of Telling Them*. Photos by Robert A. Lisak. New York, Doubleday, 1986.

A collection of personal experience stories, and guidance on the occasions for telling them. This is designed chiefly for grandparents who wish to pass on Christian moral values through storytelling.

Participation Stories for the Young Child

Carlson, Bernice Wells. *Listen! and Help Tell the Story*. Nashville, TN, Abingdon, 1965.

This is full of finger plays and poems, action verses and stories, and stories and story-poems with sound effects that children can imitate or echo. I particularly like the story "Just Like Brownie."

Jones, Bessie, and Bess Lomax Hawes. *Step It Down: Games, Plays, Songs and Stories from the Afro-American Heritage*. New York, Harper & Row, 1972.

As mentioned in Part Two, Bessie Jones is a gifted storyteller, singer, and game player from St. Simon's Island off the coast of Georgia. In this collection, one can read about her philosophy of the moral and educational value passed on through these games, stories, and songs. Also, there are many examples given in such a way that one could learn them well enough to use them with children and young people. Someday I would like to try out "Peep, Squirrel" and "Pretty Pear Tree."

Mother Goose

There are so many fine editions of Mother Goose that it would take pages and pages to list them. I recommend that parents or other adults select a favorite edition. It is usually a good idea to look at a wide variety of them, either in a public library or in a well-stocked bookstore that specializes in children's books, before making a purchase.

Use the book and pictures to accompany the recitation of the rhymes at first, but then try to say them orally, without help from the book. Use them at every opportunity you can, from age one to five. Work up from the shorter, simpler ones to those that are more complex. Encourage the child to say them along with you. They are an important part of every child's linguistic development.

Ring A Ring O' Roses. Flint Public Library, 1026 E. Kearsley, Flint, MI 48502.

Again, there are many fine books of finger plays and action rhymes that one can locate in the public library or at bookstores. But this collection is inexpensive, very extensive, and the most useful for any adult who likes acting out simple rhymed story poems with young children.

Traditional Folk and Fairy Tales

The Gateway to Storyland: Favorite Nursery Stories and Poems. Edited by Watty Piper. New York, Platt and Munk, 1985.

This collection of traditional stories for children has had many editions. It can generally be found in mass-market stores as well as in bookstores. The versions are quite tellable, but the language has been sweetened up and prettified a bit. This is for those parents who want only sweetness and light in their young child's life.

The Helen Oxenbury Nursery Story Book. New York, Alfred A. Knopf, 1985.

An excellent compilation of ten of the best traditional folk and fairy tales to begin telling or reading aloud to the child between two and four years of age. Most of the old favorites are here: "The Three Bears," "The Three Little Pigs," "Henny Penny," "The Gingerbread Boy," etc. The language here is closer to the original recorded folk tales, and full of the repetitive refrains that little children like so much.

Hurwitz, Johanna. "String Beans." in *Busybody Nora*. New York, William Morrow, 1976, pp. 47–53.

This hilarious chapter in a novel for young children should be read by any parent or grandparent who would like to know how to insert his or her own version of a favorite old story into daily life. The retelling of "Jack and the Beanstalk" is just right for the occasion when children don't want to eat their green beans. Another very effective reworking of a tale can be found in *A*

Celebration of American Family Folklore (listed above), on pages 127–128. In that case, a single parent uses her own version of "The Three Bears" to help her child cope with the divorce of her parents. However, she does this only after first using the traditional version.

McDonald, Margaret Read. *Twenty Tellable Tales*. New York, H.W. Wilson, 1985.

Although mainly intended for teachers and librarians, this collection is also very helpful for any adult who is a beginning storyteller and wishes to learn how to tell folk tales to children. The author gives very detailed notes on how she tells each story for greatest effectiveness, and much background information on each story. My favorites are "Coyote's Crying Song" and "Parley Garfield and the Frogs."

The Old-Fashioned Storybook. Selected by Betty Ann Schwartz and Leon Archibald. New York, Julian Messner, 1985.

A newly illustrated (but in nineteenth-century style) collection of twenty of the best-known fairy tales that should be introduced to children after they have become thoroughly familiar with the stories in the Oxenbury book. Generally, these are most enjoyed in the period from about five years to nine years.

Pogrebin, Letty Cottin. *Stories for Free Children*. New York, Ms. Foundation for Education and Communications, 1976.

Part One, called "Fables and Fairy Tales for Everyday Life," has a selection of stories that are nonsexist and nonviolent. The emphasis is on women and girls who are strong, individual characters.

Shannon, George. *Stories to Solve*. New York, Greenwillow, 1985.

Fourteen short tales drawn from world folklore, each with a question to answer or a puzzle to solve at the end. My favorites here are "The Sticks of Truth" and "Heaven and Hell."

Stories Using Handkerchiefs and/or Paper Cutting and Folding

Adair, Ian. *Papercrafts*. New York, Arco, 1975.

This gives no stories, but the instructions for such figures as a yacht, elephant, fish, rabbit, hats, and various other items could well inspire a story in the hands of an imaginative person.

Bauer, Caroline Feller. *Handbook for Storytellers*. Chicago, American Library Association, 1977.

Most of the advice here is geared to librarians and teachers. However, a family storyteller could use the "Fold-and-Cut Stories" on pages 306–310, as well as a number of other storytelling ideas scattered throughout the book.

Hawkesworth, Eric. *Papercutting: For Storytelling and Entertainment*. New York, S.G. Phillips, 1977.

Very clear diagrams are given for a number of paper figures, including several with story outlines.

Lewis, Shari. *Making Easy Puppets*. New York, E. P. Dutton, 1967.

This includes instructions for three handkerchief puppets. I enjoyed doing "Coppelia, the Dancing Handkerchief," while telling a little about the story behind the ballet *Coppelia*.

Lewis, Shari, and Lillian Oppenheimer. *Folding Paper Puppets*. New York, Stein and Day, 1962.

This has a number of folded-paper figures that are very suitable for storytelling. I especially like "Chatterbox," "The Talking Fish," "Big Mouth," and "Snap Dragon." The text gives only hints of stories. Most of them must be made up on the spur of the moment by the person forming the figures. However, the titles and figures are so graphic, it is not difficult to come up with short tales. They would also be good to encourage children to tell stories using the characters. For those interested, there is also an excellent article and bibliography on origami by Lillian Oppenheimer, who founded and heads the Origami Center.

Oppenheimer, Lillian, and Natalie Epstein. *More Decorative Napkin Folding*. New York, Dover Publications, 1984.

This inexpensive book is intended for the host or hostess who wishes to make clever napkin folds for a dinner party. However, a number of them, such as "Babushka," "Sunbonnet Sue," and "The Turban," seem perfect starting points for adults who wish to invent tales to go with the figures. These could be used with handkerchiefs as well as napkins.

Schimmel, Nancy. *Just Enough to Make a Story*. 2nd ed. Sisters' Choice Press, 2027 Parker St., Berkeley, CA 94704, 1982.

The story "The Handsome Prince," included here with all its instructions, is one of the most ingenious origami stories ever. It is especially effective for mixed family groups of adults and older children. A paper-tearing version of the story I call "The Captain from Krakow" is here called "The Rainhat." It has a little girl as its central character. This handbook also contains lists of "Stories to Tell to Adults" and "Active Heroines in Folktales for Children."

Warren, Jean. *Cut and Tell: Scissors Stories for Fall, 1984.*
———. *Cut and Tell: Scissors Stories for Winter, 1984.*
———. *Cut and Tell: Scissors Stories for Spring, 1984.*
All published and distributed by Totline Press, P.O. Box 2255, Everett, WA 98203.

Each of these manuals gives short stories to tell while cutting out forms from ordinary paper plates. They are meant for very young children, but one could use many of the ideas to make up stories to fit a particular family situation. I personally would like to try "Mr. Snowman's Ride" and "The Wishing Fish" from the Winter volume, and "Two Young Birds" from the Spring volume.

Drawing Stories

Mallett, Jerry J., and Marian R. Bartch. *Stories to Draw.* Freline, Inc., P.O. Box 889, Hagerstown, MD 21740. 1982.

While the authors intended this for classroom use, it would be equally useful in a family storytelling session. I like the story "Planet Y," since there are so few tellable science-fiction stories for the very young.

Oldfield, Margaret. *Tell and Draw Stories, 1963.*
———. *More Tell and Draw Stories, 1969.*
———. *Lots More Tell and Draw Stories, 1973.*
All published and distributed by Creative Storytime Press, P.O. Box 572, Minneapolis, MN 55440.

All three of these volumes show simple stories that require only a sheet of paper and a pencil or pen. The outline drawings are so easy, even a rank beginner can manage them. My personal choices are "Two Little Bugs" in the first volume; "Whale's Peace Pipe" in the second; and "Egbert the Fox" in the third. After looking at all of these examples, most adults should be able to dream up their own drawing stories, to suit the particular child or children to whom they are telling.

Pellowski, Anne. *The Story Vine*. New York, Macmillan, 1984.

Part Two includes six picture-drawing stories: two that are known worldwide, two from Japan, and two from Australia.

Stories Using Objects

Brooks, Robert J. *The Ring Snake: A Tangram Tale*. Cottage Industries, Box 244, Cobalt, CT 06414.

Tangrams are geometrical shapes that, when put together in the correct order, form a square. They are also used by the Chinese to make pictures, by moving the shapes to create human and animal figures. The game of tangrams is centuries old in China, and is played with either wooden or paper shapes. The story outlined here is a traditional one, and the instructions are fairly clear. Tangrams can often be found in Chinese gift shops, but they can easily be made from cardboard.

Gryski, Camilla. *Many Stars and More String Games*. New York, William Morrow, 1985. Toronto, Kids Can Press, 1985.

Very clear instructions are given for twenty-two figures. Stories are given for only three: "Maui's Lasso," "Maui and the Mud Hens," and "The Reluctant Sun." However, one can use many of the other figures to make up stories spontaneously. The author also did an earlier book of string figures: *Cat's Cradle, Owl's Eyes*.

Pellowski, Anne. *The Story Vine*. New York, Macmillan, 1984.

Part One contains eight string stories; Part Three has a selection of stories to tell with dolls or figurines; and Part Six gives two African stories to tell with musical instruments.

Roberts, Lynda. *Mitt Magic*. New York, Gryphon House, 1985.

Story rhymes based on the use of five fingers, with suggestions for tiny fingertip figures to attach when reciting or telling.

Stories to Tell around the Campfire, by Candlelight, or in the Dark

Almoznino, Albert. *The Art of Hand Shadows*. New York, Stravon Educational Press, 1970.

In the nineteenth century, a popular entertainment was to shape the hands in different ways, in front of a light, thereby throwing shadows on the wall. There is quite a bit of evidence to show that this was used to accompany the telling of folk tales; the wolf in Little Red Riding Hood looks truly menacing when projected in this way. This book has instructions for many hand-shadow figures that could be shown while telling a spooky story.

Brunvand, Jan Harold. *The Choking Doberman and Other Urban Folktales.* New York, W. W. Norton, 1984.
———. *The Vanishing Hitchhiker.* New York, W. W. Norton, 1981.
　　These two collections are only for older children and adults, because they are full of truly scary, bizarre, and horrific stories. However, for those who insist on a truly scary tale, this is where to find it.

Cohen, Daniel. *Southern Fried Rat and Other Gruesome Tales.* New York, M. Evans, 1983.
　　This has many of the same stories as the Brunvand collections, but they have been somewhat edited for the young listener. However, they are gruesome and not for the fainthearted.

Storytelling Events

UNITED STATES AND CANADA

There are so many storytelling events going on throughout North America that it would take a book to describe them all.

The best places to find out about the storytelling events going on at any given time in any given area are:

1. Your local public library
2. The National Association for the Preservation and Perpetuation of Storytelling (NAPPS), P.O. Box 309, Jonesborough, TN 37659. Telephone: 615-753-2171.
   NAPPS publishes an annual guide to storytelling performances, as well as a journal and newsletter devoted entirely to the subject.

There are annual festivals or conferences in the following states: Alabama, California (Bay Area and the Sierra Area), Colorado, Connecticut, District of Columbia, Florida, Georgia, Illinois, Indiana, Iowa, Kentucky, Maryland, Massachusetts, Michigan, Missouri, New Mexico, New York (Long Island, Ithaca, and NYC), North Carolina, Ohio, Oklahoma, Pennsylvania, Tennessee, Texas, and Virginia. Regional events include the Great Lakes International Storytelling Festival, Northlands Annual Storytelling Conference, Congress on New England Storytelling, and Southwest Storytelling Festival. There are events focusing on one particular group, such as the National Festival of Black Storytelling; and events centered on a specific theme, such as the annual "Clever Gretchen" Storytelling Festival at Syracuse University.

Many small groups or guilds of storytellers meet regularly in specific locales, offering each other the opportunity to exchange stories and storytelling methods. Some of them open up their sessions to visitors. For a more complete listing, consult the *National Directory of Storytelling* published by NAPPS, as well as issues of *The Yarnspinner* and *The National Storytelling Journal*.

These are just a few of the better-known or more unusual events. The information was culled from pamphlets or flyers sent to the author by the organizers, or from listings in *The Yarnspinner*. The author cannot assume responsibility for incorrect information. Check with the addresses given, or with NAPPS, for further information.

National Storytelling Festival (First weekend in October)
NAPPS, P.O. Box 309, Jonesborough, TN 37659.
About 5,000 persons converge on the town of Jonesborough for this event each year. Storytelling goes on in tents and outdoors, in the graveyard and in motel rooms, and wherever more than two persons are gathered.

Bay Area Storytelling Festival (April)
c/o Nancy Lenz, 2808 Hillegass Avenue, Berkeley, CA 94705.
Under this title or others, the festival has been an annual event in the area for at least a dozen years.

Winter Tales (Ongoing, December through March)
North Columbia Schoolhouse Cultural Center, 17894 Tyler-Foote Crossing Road, Nevada City, CA 95959.

Annual Storytelling Conference (March)
Norma Livo, University of Colorado at Denver, 1100 14th St., Denver, CO 80202.
This well-run conference has been going on for more than twelve years.

Connecticut Storytelling Festival (May)
Barbara Reed, Department of Education, Connecticut College, New London, CT 06320.

Annual Elva Young Van Winkle Storytelling Festival (November)
District of Columbia Public Library, 901 G St. NW, Washington, DC 20001.

Olde Christmas Storytelling Festival (early January)
Callanwolde Arts Center, 980 Briarcliff Road, NE, Atlanta, GA 30306.

Copper Beech Tree Storytellers' Festival (July)
Pat Craig, Arlington Heights Memorial Library, 500 N. Dunton Ave.
Arlington Heights, IL 60004.

Cedar River Storytellers' Festival (September)
Marion Gremmels, Wartburg College, 222 Ninth St. NW, Waverly, IA 50677.

Corn Island Storytelling Festival (September)
Joy Pennington, 11905 Lilac Way, Middletown, KY 40243.

Voices in the Glen Storytelling Festival (September)
Sharon Butler, 4757 Chevy Chase Drive, Chevy Chase, MD 20815.

Storytellers in Concert (usually October through May)
Lee Ellen Marvin, P.O. Box 994, Cambridge, MA 02238.
This group usually has an annual festival and congress, as well.

Great Lakes International Storytelling Festival (July)
In the past, this has been held at the state fairgrounds.

Northlands Storytelling Network Annual Conference (April)
The site changes each year. For more information write: P.O. Box 758, Minneapolis, MN 55440.

St. Louis Storytelling Festival (May)
Nan Kammann, University of Missouri-St. Louis, 8001 Natural Bridge Rd., St. Louis, MO 63121.
This festival is in its eight year and still growing.

Storytelling Institute (May)
Palmer School of Library and Information Science, C.W. Post Campus, Long Island Univ., Greenvale, NY 11548.
One of the longest-running institutes, now in its twenty-third year.

Long Island Storytelling Festival (July)
Cartoon Opera, P.O. Box 354, Huntington, NY 11743.

Clever Gretchen Conference (November)
School of Information Studies, Huntington Hall, Syracuse University, Syracuse, NY 13210.
A conference on folklore, literature, and storytelling that focuses on counteracting sexism in these areas.

Oklahoma City Winter Tales (January)
Arts Council of Oklahoma City, 400 West California St., Oklahoma City, OK 73102.

The National Festival of Black Storytelling
6653 Sprague St., Philadelphia, PA 19119

Toronto Festival of Storytelling (February)
412 A College St., Toronto, Ontario M5T 1T3 Canada.

EUROPE

There are not as many regularly scheduled storytelling events in Europe as there are in the United States and Canada. However, a number of them are so unusual, they are well worth the extra effort of planning a trip in such a way that one might attend one or more.

France

France seems to have more storytelling activity than any other nation in Europe.

Perhaps the most unusual event, and the one with the longest tradition, is the tall-tale-telling festival that occurs each August in Moncrabeau, a small village in Gascony, some 600 kilometers southwest of Paris, near the point where the Lot and Garonne rivers meet. Here, some forty local members of a "Liars' Academy" accept the challenges of local, national, and international tellers, who must register in advance. Telling is in French, of course. Usually, about twenty tellers are accepted for the final competition. Just before performing, the teller swears to *"deformer la verité et rien que la verité."*

Each teller performs in the public square, facing the forty members of the academy, dressed in their seventeenth-century outfits. Townspeople and visitors sit behind them, finding places where they can. Judging is done in the ancient manner, by passing out salt. That is, each member of the academy has a fixed amount of salt to pass out. If they like the teller very much, they give him or her a large portion of the salt. If they are not impressed with the teller's presentation, they dole out a meager amount of salt. The winner, crowned the "King of Liars," is the teller who ends up with the largest amount of salt, which is decided after each teller's portion is duly weighed on the town scales.

For those who understand even a bit of French, this annual weekend event provides a wonderful opportunity to see the French at their best, when they are laughing at themselves and their foibles, and all within the framework of colorful spectacle and delightful surroundings.

Another unusual performing group in France is the Centre de Littérature Orale, usually known as CLIO. Its headquarters are at 20 rue du Cardinal Pie, Chartres 28000. Bruno de la Salle, founder and director, each year guides his troupe through the performance of one or more of the great epics or cycles that were originally performed orally. In the past, they have performed the *Odyssey, Tales of Scheherazade,* and *The Search for the Grail*, among others. Their performances are usually at cathedrals or outdoor sites such as that at the Festival of Avignon. Sometimes they are videotaped and repeated on French television. For any person at all interested in the French language, or in French literature, these are "must-see" performances.

The Collectif Contes, Bibliothèques Municipales, 3 Boulevard Marechal Lyautey, Grenoble 38021, is another source of information about storytelling events, especially those in central and southern France. They publish an occasional journal, *Ouirdire*, that describes a number of special storytelling events or groups.

Family storytelling and library or institutional storytelling can be found in many parts of France on an ongoing basis. Two places to write for information as to specific events that might be taking place at any given time are:

La Joie par les Livres
8 rue Saint-Bon
Paris 75004

L'Age d'Or de France
1 rue Denis-Poisson
Paris 75017

As always, when writing for information from another country, include as a courtesy an international postal reply coupon, which you can get from any post office. It also helps if you can write your request in French, however rudimentary.

Finally, there is an annual Festival of Storytelling held by the Alliance Française in Paris each spring, generally in March. These are international festivals, and usually include a few tellers from several French-speaking African countries, as well as from such places as French Canada, Haiti, and other territories associated historically with France. The audiences are virtually all high-school-age and up. No children's stories here!

Great Britain

Many towns in England have summer folk festivals, and some have regular monthly meetings of persons with interest in folklore, ballads, and the like. Some are highly structured, but most are quite casual and free in form, and welcome participation by folk storytellers. The visitor must ask around in the areas he or she wishes to visit.

The town of Sidmouth, in Devon, is fairly typical, with its International Folk Festival each summer. One part of the festival includes storytelling, and in a manner similar to that in the French town of Moncrabeau (see above), the winner is declared "Liar in Chief." At least one American, Louise Sherman of Leonia, New Jersey, has held this honor, and returned the following summer to crown her successor, as tradition demanded. She subsequently returned to be the judge of that part of the festival!

Another group that meets regularly and is open to all listeners, for a small donation, is the College of Storytellers, Freepost, London NW3 1YB, England. This is a volunteer group, so when writing ahead to find out when and where one or more members of their group might be telling, be sure to enclose an international postal response coupon.

Denmark

One of the joys of visiting the Hans Christian Andersen Museum in summer is that there are regular storytelling performances, in Danish, English, and other languages. Unfortunately, the season is so short, one must plan carefully ahead if one wants to catch one of the better story performances. Some of them are done in theatrical form and others are simply narrated. However, the whole ambiance of the town, the ferry and train rides to get there, and the excellent facilities in and around the museum make any visit there a pleasure. Further information can be had by writing to any Danish National Tourist Office or to the Odense Tourist Association, Town Hall, Odense, Denmark.

OTHER COUNTRIES

Australia

There are storytelling guilds in most of the states of Australia. The contact addresses for two of them are:

Storytelling Guild of S. Australia
c/o Public Libraries Division
Norwood, South Australia
5067 Australia

Storytellers of Victoria
30 Madden Grove
Burnley, Victoria
3121 Australia

To get current contact addresses for the other groups, you might write to the Cultural Affairs Officer of the Australian Embassy or Consulate nearest you.

Pat Scott, one of Australia's leading tellers, runs a storytelling center in the state of Tasmania. Many of her sessions are open to outsiders, upon payment of a fee. The address for the center is P.O. Box 21, Oatlands, Tasmania, 7205 Australia.

Japan

A visit with the Ohanashi Caravan can be an unforgettable experience. This professional troupe of tellers, puppeteers, singers, and other performers was initially inspired by the Weston Woods Caravans of Morton Schindel. However, Mrs. Ishitake, the indefatigable director of the Ohanashi Caravan operations, has gone far beyond imitation. Ohanashi can arrange for visits, if they are informed well in advance. All performances are in Japanese, of course, but the material is presented to its young audiences so well that one can appreciate the results without understanding more than a word or two. The address for Ohanashi Caravan is: 1-10 Yanagikubo, Higashikurume, Tokyo, Japan.

More traditional forms of library storytelling can be observed in the Tokyo Children's Library, c/o Kiyoko Matsuoka, 3-17-10 Ehara-cho, Nakano-ku, Tokyo 165. Again, be sure to send international postal reply coupons.

Also in Tokyo, a visit to a *yose* can be quite intriguing. The yose are storytelling halls, and a few of them are still in operation in Tokyo and some other Japanese cities. The Western visitor can often arrange with a local tour guide for such a visit. Polite but persistent questioning will usually locate any yose that happen to have performances for the period one intends to be in Japan. The entry fees are modest, and one is quite free to come and go, if the tellers do not prove particularly interesting.

In the town of Kusu, in Oita Prefecture in Kyushu Island in the south of Japan, is a unique storytelling hall and children's museum. It was erected in honor of Takehiko Kurushima, known as the Andersen of Japan. It is far off the beaten path of the usual tourists to Japan. Storytelling festivals are to be held here annually. For more information, write to the Children and Family Division, Social Welfare Department, Oita Prefectural Government, 3-1-1 Ohtemachi, Oita 870, Japan.

Miscellaneous

There are numerous storytelling events in other countries, but rarely on a regular basis. If you are going to a particular country and wish to see one or more storytellers in action, the best tactic is to search through catalogs and indexes in large university libraries for books and articles published by anthropologists, folklorists, and others who have studied storytelling in that particular country. Often, a letter to such a scholar, stating your interest and indicating your desire to observe a teller or tellers in action, will bring a positive and helpful response. Again, don't forget the stamped, self-addressed envelope.